We Are Legion

by Robert Whitmore
Copyright 2024

We Are Legion

Other books by Robert Whitmore:

What Others Won't Do
Cain: St. Louis

1

Bonnie Rose sped along the main aisle of the distribution center in her gray forklift. She had a perfect safety record, but also knew that everyone else would have parked for the day. Getting a promotion was tough, so she tried to pick at least one extra order at the end of each of her ten-hour shifts. Impressing the boss seemed like the best way to move up the ladder.

The hard, rubber tires of the forklift squealed on the waxed concrete floor as she turned toward the area where the drivers parked. Hers had a black six painted on its side. She backed it into the spot with a matching six on the wall. The maintenance team would give it a quick look and refill the propane tank before she came back.

Bonnie saw small blue picking carts rushing around at the far end of the warehouse. It had taken her five years of filling those orders before she had convinced her manager to give her a shot at an opening as a forklift driver. She unbuckled herself, checked all the switches one more time, and then got down. It was a great relief to feel her hard hat come off. She shook out her sandy blonde hair, letting it fall to her shoulders.

"Hey, Bonnie," said a man in brown coveralls. He was standing in front of forklift number three. His wavy red hair would grab anyone's attention. "Jimmy wants everyone in the meeting room in five minutes."

"Thanks, Chuck," she said. His name was Bernard, but everyone in the warehouse called him Chuck, although she didn't know why. Bonnie gathered her hair into her right hand and used the left to slip a white hair tie around it. She liked wearing a ponytail, but it did not work well with her hard hat. "This better be good. Jimmy knows it is quitting time."

Impromptu meetings did not work well with taking an extra order. She could see everyone shuffling into the meeting room but made a quick trip to the bathroom.

Everyone had taken a seat by the time she came in, so she slid into one of the orange, molded plastic chairs at the back. It was a fancy name for a room with five worn out tables and three vending machines that were rarely more than half stocked.

"I'll start by saying that I know you're all ready to get out of here," Jimmy said as soon as he stepped in the room, holding a manilla envelope. The word 'Inter-Office' was printed in bold, black lettering on the outside. His hair had gone from jet black when Bonnie started to a blend of gray and black. That day it was a mess. He ran his fingers through it again, showing exactly why it was out of place. She noticed he had bags under his eyes, something she had never seen before.

"You got that right!" shouted Tom Bryant, drawing laughter from the other workers. He stood over six and half feet tall and was surprisingly strong for a man in his early sixties. She shook her head at him, but he only offered a shrug in return. Tom had become something of a father figure to Bonnie over the years.

"Okay, Tom," Jimmy said with a forced laugh, but Bonnie could tell that there was no joy in it. "I'm going to get right down to it. About an hour ago, Todd Schnurberg, the CEO, signed a contract with a third party to handle their distribution. The union lawyers are working on it right now, but it looks like they can pull it off since the workers will not be company employees."

"What exactly does that mean for us?" Chuck asked. His face had paled, standing in sharp contrast to his red hair. All happiness about the workday being over had been sucked from the room.

"It means that we have three weeks left here," Jimmy said, holding up the envelope. "They have apparently been working on this for a while, but I didn't know about it until the announcement today. Frankly, I'm pissed, but I don't know what we can do about it. The new company is offering jobs to anyone who wants one, but the pay will be about two-thirds of our current rate with no benefits of any kind."

"How can they do that?" Tom asked, his thick arms crossed across his chest. "What are you going to do, Jimmy?"

"I'm not a lawyer, but it sure sounds like they found a loophole in the contract, and they are exploiting it to the max. The official statement says that it is 'just part of doing business'."

"I'd like to show them how to do business," Chuck said. Others groaned in agreement.

"As for your second question, Tom, I'm going to be out looking for something else. The prospects aren't good for a guy in his late forties, but I can't take that kind of pay cut and lose my benefits. I'm eighteen months from my twenty-five years but going to the new center doesn't help because I wouldn't be a Schnurberg employee. It's a giant cluster."

"Only for us!" Tom exclaimed. "The people on high will probably get a healthy bonus for cutting expenses."

"I wish I wasn't the one to have to tell you," Jimmy said, "but we all know none of the big dogs are going to set foot in here while we are here."

"They know we'd tear them apart!" Chuck yelled, rising out of his chair and shaking his fist.

Bonnie slowly twisted the lid of her water bottle on and off as she listened. The anger in the room built all around her, but the conversation faded into background noise as she started thinking about what was coming. She had never been one to have a quick temper. However, everyone knew she was capable of handling business if someone pushed her far enough. For the last hour of her shift, she had been thinking of nothing but getting home, showering, and crawling in bed. Now, considering she lived paycheck to paycheck, she was trying to decide where that bed would be in a few weeks.

She had moved into a one bedroom, one bath apartment on the southside of St. Louis three months earlier. The move had happened because her long-time roommate, Lisa, had moved to New York. She made reasonable money working at the distribution center but had to give up the nice loft downtown once she had no one to split living costs with. Now, she was using all her income to stay afloat between her apartment, car maintenance, and student loans.

Bonnie didn't hear Jimmy offer to buy the first round at Southtown Pub, but she wouldn't have gone anyway. She liked going out to celebrate and have fun. Drinking away her sorrows was not on the agenda.

"What's on your mind?" Tom asked, bringing Bonnie out of her trance. Everyone else was leaving the room.

"Same as you, I imagine."

"I guess so," he said, sitting in the chair across the table from her. His long legs stretched out to his right instead of folding under the table. "I'm guessing our situations aren't exactly the same though."

"Well, I'm not a sixty-something man," she said with a forced grin.

"True, but I was thinking more along the lines of finances."

"I bet we aren't the same there either," she said. The fake smile was long gone as she looked down at her water bottle.

"You might be surprised. No one is going to want to hire a warehouse worker my age, and my savings are exhausted."

"You've been here forever! Can't you retire and draw something or other."

"Sure, I could get social security and maybe some sort of Medicare. Truth is, though, that I can't pay my bills with that."

"I don't mean to pry, but how can that be?" she asked.

"It's fine," he said. "About a year before you started here, my wife was killed in a car accident."

"Yeah, you told me that a long time ago."

"What I didn't tell you is that she owned her own little hair salon. The life insurance policy we had ended up not being enough to cover her final expenses. We didn't have any children, so we had never worried too much about that sort of thing. There was enough in savings to cover the difference, but I soon found out that the salon was barely breaking even, and I knew nothing about doing hair," he said, patting the top of his bald head. "It wasn't that she didn't tell me about the situation at the shop. She made enough to keep the bills paid at home, so I never asked. It took months to sell the building, and no one was willing to buy the business itself, so that was all sunk costs. I found another salon that was finally willing to buy her supplies, but for pennies on the dollar. In the end, my poor planning wiped out all but four thousand dollars."

"Geez," Bonnie said, looking up at Tom. "I mean, I don't know what I'm going to do, but my problems seem pretty minor now."

"Nah, that's not what I was trying to say. Having your basic needs met is what every person should have, no matter your situation."

"I guess that's where I'm at now. I don't have savings and I am not sure what I'll find that can match what I was making here."

"I'd offer to let you stay with me, but I sold my house last year to try and reduce expenses. Unfortunately, it wasn't in the best neighborhood, and I didn't get much for it. I was planning to work until seventy and then hope for the best. I'm staying in an efficiency apartment above a deli on Kingshighway."

"I'm guessing we're both in bad shape," Bonnie said.

"Do you have family to stay with if you don't find something else?"

"No, I'm a foster kid. I had a good placement until I was twelve, but then my foster mom got really sick, and I had to go back into the system. The next five years I bounced around and finally got emancipated at seventeen. I was able to get some financial aid, but college was expensive. I was determined not to stay down. It went pretty well until my internship after college failed to turn into a full time job and I came here."

"You're a hard worker, Bonnie, we all know that. You are the first female forklift driver we've had and that's saying something."

"The one bright spot is that we have three weeks left to figure something out," she said. "It just sucks that they dropped this on us on a Friday."

An hour later, Bonnie flopped onto her couch and stared at the ceiling. She thought about making some dinner but couldn't work up the desire to eat anything. A frozen pizza or leftover chili would usually make her mouth water after work, but neither sounded good that night. She couldn't even stomach the idea of a simple salad. The stress was overwhelming.

The rest of the weekend was pretty much the same. She tried searching online for anything that could pay the bills. She looked at combining part-time positions and others that offered plenty of overtime. Thirty-six resumes went out for jobs that were mediocre at best. The frustration pushed the limits of what she could handle. She steadied herself, knowing that she still had three weeks of good income.

On Monday at two-thirty, she drove her black Ford Fusion onto the lot of the distribution center. She stopped the car just after clearing the main gate and stared at the building. There were usually five or six trailers waiting to be loaded during her shift, but she saw that all twelve bays were occupied. In seven years, she had never seen that. She wondered if maybe the plan had fallen through, and work was picking up instead.

She parked her car under a maple tree that had already dropped its leaves. Two spots over, a four-door F-150 was backed in. It was spotless, and Bonnie was glad to know that Tom was already there. They were never allowed to clock in early, so she figured that he would be waiting on one of the picnic tables at the side of the building on that unseasonably warm afternoon.

Sure enough, he was at a table pushed up against the building, giving him a spot in the shade. He was engrossed in whatever story he was reading in the newspaper. Bonnie slid onto the bench opposite him.

"Lot of trailers out there, huh," he said without looking up. Bonnie smiled.

"I was going to tell you that. Any idea what's going on?"

"Who knows? They are probably getting more shipments in to prepare for the new building. Jimmy said the new place is about fifty percent bigger than this one. I guess they can support a bigger building since they don't have to pay the workers," he said. The corner of his mouth turned up. His eyes remained focused on the paper.

"I guess maybe we can get some overtime or something, then."

"More likely that they will want us to get more done in the same amount of time."

Bonnie shook her head, knowing that he was right. "Anything worth reading in the news today?"

"Not worth reading but disturbing all the same. Apparently, the new mayor's first step in improving downtown is to get rid of the homeless people."

"Right," Bonnie said sarcastically, "that's the real problem."

"The mayor seems to think that gun violence and robberies are being committed by only the homeless people. She says that businesses are not interested in locating downtown because of them. A total load of shit if you ask me."

"I'm with you on that," Bonnie commented. "Back to those trucks, though."

"I guess we'll find out in about fifteen minutes. I saw Jimmy pull in minutes before you, so there will probably be some sort of meeting to greet us first thing on this fine Monday."

"Can you spare the sports section?"

Tom flipped back a couple sections and removed the part with 'Sports' plastered across the header. Bonnie started glancing through, reading about the baseball playoffs, which did not feature her beloved Cardinals. Then, she read a little about the Blues and some commentary on the NFL season, which she did not care much about.

"I'm going to head in," Tom said. "I need to visit the little boys' room before we get started."

"I'll go with you," Bonnie said. "Well, not to the little boys' room."

Tom chuckled and folded up his paper. Bonnie added the sports section to his pile, and they walked around the corner to the main entrance of the building. A piece of plain white paper was taped to the door saying that there would be a staff meeting at 3:05.

The members of the second shift were in their normal spots when Jimmy walked in. Everyone looked dejected, which was understandable. The regular chit chat was nonexistent.

"So," Jimmy said, taking a seat at one of the tables, "I'm not even going to pretend that I want to be here. I'm sure most of you don't either. Sometimes they call it throwing you a curveball, but I'd describe this more as a bean ball."

Everyone was listening intently. The tension was palpable.

"The bays were full of trailers when I got here, which I'm sure you all noticed. I had a memo waiting in my bin that

I could not have expected. It appears that they want to empty out this facility by Wednesday," Jimmy said. A general sigh could be heard around the room as most people shook their heads. "They are really putting it to us."

"Why the change?" Chuck asked. "I was counting on three more weeks of work."

"A guy I know at the main office said they secured a renter for this building, but they need it by next week," Jimmy answered. "So, of course, money talks."

"Can they do that?" Tom asked, sounding anything but hopeful.

"I asked them what happens if we aren't done by Wednesday. I was told that if we aren't done, they will go ahead and terminate our contracts anyway. Then, they'll bring in a third party to finish the loadout."

"Ridiculous," Bonnie said.

"I wish there was something I could do," Jimmy said, placing his palms flat on the table and looking out at his workers, people he considered something close to family.

"No one is upset with you Jimmy," Bonnie said. "You are in the same boat as we are."

"Still doesn't make it okay, Bonnie," he replied. "I will say that I've heard there is a temp agency that is looking to hire warehouse workers in North County."

"I talked to them this weekend," Chuck said. "No benefits at all and the pay doesn't touch what we had here."

"Probably hiring for the jobs at the new facility," Tom offered.

"Most likely," Jimmy said. "I guess we can only go out there and get three good days in and hope for the best. Before we finish, I want everyone to leave a good phone number for me so I can stay in touch. Especially if I come across some openings somewhere."

Each worker wrote down their name and number before heading out into the warehouse. The pickers shifted from their normal duty of filling small orders to sealing up partially used boxes. The forklift drivers were each assigned an aisle and a pair of trucks that they started loading. There was no laughter or crude humor in the air that day. The place felt more like a wake than a normal shift.

At 11:35 on Wednesday night, Bonnie took her lunch box and jacket out of her locker for the last time. Everyone else did the same thing before wandering out into the parking lot. They all stood there for two or three minutes, trying to figure out what to say.

"I'm going to miss you all," Tom said, surprising everyone. "You've basically been my family for the last few years. I hope we can stay in touch, but I know how these things go."

Others followed with similar commentary. By midnight, they were all pulling out of the lot. The lone pole light near the main entrance was the only break in the darkness. Jimmy pushed open the door several minutes later and looked up at the light. He had hoped to catch everyone before they left, but his boss had called right when the shift ended. He leaned back in the door and flipped a switch that killed that one glowing presence.

2

Friday afternoon, Bonnie was sitting at her kitchen table looking at employment websites. Indeed, Monster, and CareerBuilder all had dozens of listings, but she probably wouldn't qualify for the jobs that paid enough to cover her bills. Between jobs, she would flip back over to her bank account and stare, wondering how she was going to make it through the rest of the month. Her former employer had escaped paying severance by saying that the workers were offered positions at the new facility, but they had declined. The union would help by providing a small percentage of their pay for a month, but anything beyond that was completely unknown.

She had talked to Tom once, but he hadn't found any leads that were worthwhile. They agreed that the 'Right to Work' legislation that the new governor had pushed was making it really hard to make a decent wage in Missouri. Then again, the corporations that helped elect him were raking in major savings by hiring non-union workers and not offering any more benefits than required by the federal mandate. Her phone rang.

"Hello."

"Hey, Bonnie, it's Bernard."

"Who?" she said, thinking. "Oh, hey, Chuck. Is it okay if I still call you that?"

"Sure, whatever, just don't call me late for dinner."

"Good one. What's up?"

"Just wanted to let you know I found a place that is buying used furniture and household goods if you are looking to sell anything. I'm clearing out my place. I'm only keeping what will fit in my truck, which isn't much. I found a short term gig in eastern Kansas doing cleanup for a factory that burned down last year. Should be three to four months. I can try to get you hired on, but they said it was one spot only."

"Thanks anyway, Chuck, don't jeopardize your spot by pushing for me. If you get there and they have an opening, let me know. I'll take the info on that place buying furniture. I might as well sell what I can. If I have to move, I sure can't fit this stuff in my car."

She took the information and made a call. The contact offered her close to two thousand dollars for her stuff, leaving her with only a handful of small items in her apartment. She could pay bills for a couple extra months with that money, but she still knew it was not a good fix.

The weekend was painfully long. Bonnie slept through most of it. She woke up on Monday morning, thinking that maybe she would go ahead and take the forklift job at the new facility. It would be something at least, although it would still leave her without enough money for rent and bills in six months. She was sitting on her kitchen floor eating a piece of buttered toast with a cup of cheap coffee when her phone rang.

"Tom?" she said, looking at the caller ID.

"Hey, kiddo. How was your weekend?"

"Oh, it was a blast," she said, smiling for the first time in a week.

"Same here," he said. "Heard about any jobs?"

"Not really. I'm thinking about taking one of the jobs at the new facility."

"Nah, don't do that. You'd hate it and probably just be pissed at yourself for crossing that line."

"I know, but I've got to have something."

"Heard from anyone else?"

"Just Chuck, he found some sort of job in Kansas doing industrial cleanup."

"Sounds awful," Tom said. "Are you going with him?"

"Ha, no. I don't even think there is a job for me out there, if I went."

"I'm not sure if you'd be interested, but I found a short term gig southeast of Springfield."

"Doing what?"

"End of season maintenance at a corporate farm. They need workers, so I thought I'd check in with you."

"Sure," she said. "I need to do something and staring at these walls is going to make me crazy. How's the pay?"

"Three thousand in cash for a month and they provide lodging. No benefits though."

"That's a big step up from going to the new facility. What are you going to do after the month?"

"Who knows," he said. "I'll worry about that next month. I'm hoping that there will be more opportunities in Springfield or Joplin than there are here."

"When do we leave?"

"They want me there by Thursday morning, but I'll probably head down there tomorrow. Want to ride with me?"

"I might as well follow in my car. I don't have anywhere to leave it here."

"Fair enough. I'll meet you at Uncle Bill's for breakfast tomorrow at 8. My treat and then we will take off."

"You don't have to buy my…"

"Stop there," he said firmly. "I'm buying your breakfast. Don't argue with me young lady."

She laughed and they talked some more. Bonnie spent the rest of the day putting her last few things in boxes and loading her car. It was amazing how much life had changed in under two weeks, but at least she had a good friend to go with into the unknown.

3

Bonnie, Tom, and a half dozen others were standing in a mobile office trailer on that Thursday morning. It was crowded, but no one minded because they were thankful for the work. A woman wearing faded green coveralls was sitting at the built-in desk in what looked like a second hand swivel chair. Her black hair was in a ponytail that was tucked through the back of a ballcap. Cool blue eyes studied the group for a moment.

"Welcome to you all," she said with a smile. "My name is Chrissy Dunphy. I'm in charge of this show. It is going to be hard work and we are on a definite deadline. If you look out the window to your right, you'll see a steel shed. Large does not cover it, since it is five hundred feet long and a hundred feet deep. There is another identical shed about twenty yards behind it. Both buildings are full of farm implements. Tractors, wagons, combines, plows, disks, planters, and so on. Each piece needs to be ready to go to auction within three weeks. This will require some serious elbow grease. We will also be disassembling the four grain bins that you can see out the left window. That should go a little more quickly but will still be hard work. We are hoping that winds stay down during that part of the project. Today, since it is drizzling a little, we will go to the first shed and start working. There are plenty of brushes, sprayers, and other cleaning supplies waiting for you. We will provide lunch at noon, and we will shuttle you all back to the motel promptly at 6. Tomorrow, we will pick you up again at 6 am to do it all over again. Any questions?"

"Why is all of this being sold?"

"My company's client is a major bank. They repossessed the property along with all of the equipment when the farmer defaulted on his loans this fall. He had leveraged everything on getting a yield above what was considered likely, and he lost. It's just business, nothing personal. I'm not a big fan of this sort of thing. But, as most of you know, a good job can be hard to come by. Anything else?"

"So, twelve hour days?" asked a tall man with a scraggly brown beard hanging down over his flannel work shirt.

"You're Ervin, right?"

"That's me."

"Well, Ervin, the answer is yes. But only if you include your travel time in the morning, a fifteen minute break every three hours, and a thirty minute lunch."

"Sounds fair to me, but everyone calls me Erv," he said before turning to look out the left side window at the steel bins. A gigantic Pioneer sign was attached to the nearest structure.

"Great. Now, let's get to work," Chrissy said, getting to her feet. "And, yes, I will be working right alongside you in between my paperwork and conference calls. We ended up having about three less people than we actually wanted, but I think we'll make do."

The crew followed her out the door on the right side of the trailer and down a freshly built set of wooden steps. The grass had grown to a little more than ankle height but was probably done for the season. The cool weather would make it dormant very soon.

"So, what do you think?" Bonnie asked in a hushed voice as she walked with Tom.

"Not exactly what I was expecting, but it'll do."

"I've never seen a tractor in person, let alone any of the other things she said."

"Me neither, other than in fields as I went by on the interstate or something."

The shed was massive. Bonnie was sure it was bigger than the warehouse had been, although this building was open to the outside air. Four huge overhead doors were raised, and they could see the green farm equipment inside.

Erv was just behind Chrissy at the head of the pack and made his way into the building first. Bonnie and Tom brought up the end of the line.

Chrissy waited for the group to make it inside and then said, "There are water faucets next to each of the overhead doors. The hoses are on rolling reels to make your life easier. A couple hundred feet of hose can get heavy. Pressure washers are also down there, and there are some gas cans for them when you need to refill. The soaps, window cleaner, and other such things are on the steel shelf between doors one and two. If there is anything you think would make the job easier, let me know and I'll do my best to get it."

"How about a ladder?" asked one of the shorter men.

"Of course," Chrissy said. "They are against the far end of the steel shelf. Six or eight of them, I think. Be careful with them as they can be a little slippery when they get wet. All set, then?"

"Let's get'er done," Erv said, offering a smile through his shaggy beard.

"Very good. I'll be in the office if you need me," Chrissy said, and strode back out of the building.

"That's a funny way to work alongside us," Bonnie said. "Anyway, I think we should at least know each other's names. We are going to be working side by side, and I think calling each other 'hey you' sounds boring. My name is Bonnie."

"Well, you certainly aren't shy," Erv said.

"That's a fact, and my name is Tom."

"I'm Gerald, but my friends call me Giant," said the shorter man who had asked about the ladders. "This is my cousin Richard, they call him Tiny. He's a quiet guy, so don't be offended if he doesn't have much to say."

Tiny offered a short wave of his hand, which looked big enough to easily grasp the head of anyone there. Bonnie guessed he was seven feet tall and close to three hundred and fifty pounds. The worn and oversized cowboy hat on his head made him look even bigger. She was sure he would be earning his share of the pay.

"I'm still Erv."

"Michelle," said a woman of about forty with short blonde hair and a tough look on her face.

"I'm Amber and this is my husband, Ryan," said a thirtyish looking woman with curly brown hair and glasses. Ryan was a little over six feet tall and offered a silent smile with a wave.

"Are you and Tom together?" Giant asked, and immediately regretted it. "Just wondering. You don't have to tell me."

"Tom and I worked in the same warehouse back in St. Louis, and we both got screwed over by the same corporation last week. We worked together for about seven years, most recently as forklift operators. Beyond that, he's basically my dad."

Tom smiled and patted her on the back.

"How do you all want to handle this?" Amber asked. "Seems like taking on one of these machines alone would be overwhelming."

Michelle spoke up in the raspy voice of a long time smoker. "I spent a summer working for a trucking company two summers ago. They had me cleaning trucks. One person would work their way around the truck with a pressure washer and the other would use a heavy-duty broom to knock off debris. Seems like that would be a good plan here."

"I like it," Erv said.

"Let's do four machines, working in pairs. Then we can go back and tackle the detail work as a whole group," Bonnie said. "Now, what are the pairs going to be? Tiny and Giant?"

"Sure," Giant said and started off toward the supplies with Tiny following close behind.

"Amber and I will be working together," Ryan said, and the couple walked away.

"Bonnie?" Erv asked. "Who are you with?"

"I think Michelle and I would make a good team," she said, and noticed Michelle's eyes flick her way for just a moment. "You and Tom will probably have fun."

"I always have fun," Erv said.

"Me, too!" Tom said with a laugh, and the two men walked away.

"So why me?" Michelle asked as she and Bonnie headed off toward the supplies.

"I like to get to know people, and I have a feeling that you have an interesting story to tell. I already know Tom and, honestly, Erv seems to wear his soul on his sleeve."

"I don't think I'm all that interesting, but whatever," Michelle said, a satisfied look on her face.

Amber and Ryan took the twenty-four row planter on the end. Giant and Tiny took the S690 combine next to it, although the header was not attached. A pair of 9520 tractors were next in line.

"How competitive are you?" Bonnie asked Michelle in a hushed voice.

"A little too competitive sometimes."

"Hey, Tom and Erv," Bonnie said. "How about a friendly wager? Bragging rights."

"I'm in," Erv said, his perpetual smile showing. "The tractor on the left is dirtier, though. I think we will take that one. I don't want any excuses when we win."

"Not a chance," Michelle said. "You are the one who will be looking for an excuse. We will take the tractor on the left."

"So be it," Erv said, grabbing a reel of hose and starting for his machine. Tom was close behind with a pressure washer and a broom.

"Let's not beat them too bad," Michelle said, looking excited.

"Deal," Bonnie said.

It took three days to get through all the equipment in the first shed, not counting the detailing. They started with that on Saturday morning. Amber suggested working in teams of four. Bonnie and Michelle had easily won their competition against Tom and Erv, so Erv had suggested a men versus women competition on the detailing.

"Five on three doesn't seem fair," Ryan said. "I'll work on their team."

"No," Michelle said. "We don't need a martyr. We need someone who can listen to instructions and not argue. We'll take Tiny."

The big man blushed a little and smiled.

"Assuming that is okay?" Michelle asked.

"Yeah," Tiny said and turned a darker shade of crimson.

"Game on then," Erv said and started off toward the planter that Ryan and Amber had cleaned.

4

The days went by quickly. They finished off the task with a pair of grain wagons in the second shed.

"So, what do we do now?" Michelle asked.

"Maybe we can get a little break?" Erv commented with his typical grin on his face.

"That's exactly what you are all going to do," said Chrissy, who had walked in the shed while the group was looking over their handiwork. "We are officially a day and a half ahead of schedule. I talked to my boss in Cleveland, and he said you should all take the rest of the day today and all day tomorrow off. No cut in your pay or penalty of any kind. Just relax."

"Sounds too good to be true," Giant said.

"Shut it," Amber said with a laugh. "I could use a day off."

"The driver will be here with the van in about twenty minutes. I'm going to give each of you an extra twenty bucks to buy a good dinner at Ben's Roadhouse. It's probably the nicest place in town, although there isn't a lot of competition."

"Is twenty going to be enough to feed Tiny?" Erv asked, drawing a deep laugh from the big man.

"Maybe we can just throw all the cash in together and see what happens," Bonnie said.

"Sounds good to me," Tom said.

"I used to waitress at a Denny's. I can tell you that tips are hard to live on," Amber said. "How about if we all agree to leave any change for whoever waits on us."

"No argument here," Giant said.

About an hour later, they pulled into the Motel 5 parking lot. It had been a good place for the group to stay, despite the fact she had doubts when they first arrived. Michelle found the name amusing at first, but enjoyed the service provided by the owner, Gary Floyd. Gary had been the epitome of the small town business owner who does everything on their own. He even replaced a window that had broken in Bonnie's room when a deer crashed into it just after dawn.

"So, where are you all headed tonight?" Gary asked as Giant, Tiny, Tom, and Bonnie walked into the lobby.

"The eight of us are going down to Ben's Roadhouse," Bonnie said. "We are getting an unexpected vacation day tomorrow."

"Oh, yeah, Ben's is a great place," Gary said. "The wings and steaks are pretty amazing, but I'd steer clear of the roast beef. Just my humble opinion. They do have a sixty-eight ounce ribeye called The Beast that goes for $30 unless you can eat the whole thing, then it's free. Your typical gimmick menu item."

"I bet Tiny could handle that!" Michelle said from the behind them, having slipped in while Gary was talking. Tiny looked back at her and blushed.

Around nine that night, they all walked back up the asphalt driveway of Motel 5. They were laughing and Tiny was wearing a huge smile, having finished The Beast with room for dessert. Michelle had stuck to wings and beer, while the others had some variety of cheeseburgers.

They were all different but had come to enjoy their little group. The next day they settled in Amber and Ryan's room to watch a movie and eat pizza.

"So, Bonnie," Michelle said, "you and Tom worked together in St. Louis?"

"Sure did," Bonnie said. "We worked in a distribution center for a grocery store called Schnurberg's. Where are you from?"

"I've kind of drifted around, but I grew up in Kirksville. My dad was an associate professor at Truman until my sophomore year in college. I was doing the free ride thing since he was an employee, but funding got cut and so did his job. I took a job in a box store, hated it. Then, I went to

KC to work for a bank, hated it. Finally started backpacking around the country doing odd jobs. It's a hard way to get by, but at least I'm happy."

"This is you being happy?" Erv asked.

"Shut up, Erv," she said. "What's your story, anyway?"

"Nothing fancy. Just a guy who lost his job at a meatpacking plant in Green Bay about two years ago and has been exploring the Midwest since then. I worked for a long distance home moving company for a while, but that was boring. I keep thinking I'll land a gig as a model."

Everyone laughed at the joke. Erv swung his arms like he had just hit a homerun in the bottom of the ninth of a playoff game. He threw his hands up in celebration.

"Okay, okay," Tom said. "It wasn't that funny. Has anyone thought about where they are going next week or what they might be doing?"

"That sounds a lot like responsible adult talk to me," Giant said. "How about we just watch Caddyshack?"

The movie had just started and the gopher was doing his infamous little dance in the golf course, preparing to torment Bill Murray. Kenny Loggins was singing 'I'm Alright'. Erv, Amber, and Bonnie all started singing along as soon as the chorus came up.

The absurdity continued for a while, and all eight of them were entranced. Bill Murray was scrubbing the bottom of the country club pool and found what the rich club members had assumed was a piece of poop. He looked it over and took a big bite.

"Aaaand on that note," Michelle said, "maybe we should get back to Tom's question. I don't have a plan past next week, but I was hoping to find something in one of the papers this week. I figured the three grand would buy me a couple days to get things lined out."

"Tiny and I are probably going to Texas with the hope of picking up something. Might even stop off in Oklahoma if the right deal reveals itself."

"I don't know what I'm going to do," Bonnie said. "I guess I can go back to St. Louis, but that situation certainly won't be any better now than it was before."

"That's a fact," Tom added. "I was looking at a copy of the Post-Dispatch this morning while I was talking with Gary. They are pushing forward on the mayor's plan to get all the homeless people out of downtown and the Right to Work legislation has taken down two more big warehouses. The only jobs available outside of technology seem to be minimum wage spots that are replacing the skilled positions."

"I guess they don't realize that can't work forever," Erv said.

"I'm sure they do," Ryan said. "The thing is that they will cash in big time until things start to fall apart. By that time there will be enough skilled people in serious need of work that they will go back for a fraction of their former pay."

"Disgusting," Michelle said. "I wish there was a way to fight back, but money talks in politics. Big business wins every time."

No one had a response for that, so they went back to watching the movie. The eight of them wasted away the rest of the afternoon eating pizza and snacks from the QT station down the road. The discussion switched back to lighter topics, allowing them to learn more about each other.

Around nine that night, they started to disperse. They still wanted to get a good night's rest, since they had no clue as to the task that waited for them the next day.

5

"Better hurry up and get something to eat," Giant said to Michelle as she walked into the cozy Motel 5 lobby. "Tiny already ate all the waffles, but there are still some eggs and cereal. Probably yogurt, too, since he doesn't really like that stuff."

Tiny shook his head with a wrinkled nose at the thought of eating yogurt.

"I'm just looking for coffee," Michelle said. "Besides, the van will be here in about five minutes."

"You should still get something to eat," Amber said from her seat at a table near the back wall.

"Yes, mother," Michelle said, stopping in front of what was left of the continental breakfast on the small faux marble countertop next to the front desk. The brass clock hanging on the wall showed that it was 5:56. Michelle cursed herself for staying in bed so long.

"Let's go everyone," Bonnie said after pushing open the glass door leading to the parking lot. "I can see the van coming up the road."

Amber and Ryan tossed the trash from their table in the domed silver can next to the door and walked outside. Tiny and Giant were close behind. Michelle popped a lid on her coffee and grabbed an apple.

Tom picked up the khaki knapsack he always carried with him. He kept his most important information and some snacks in it. The van did not slow, instead flying right by and they saw that it had 'Little Angels Daycare' painted on the side.

"You'd think that van would be here to pick us up," Giant said. "Us being a group of little angels and all."

Tiny started laughing his deep belly laugh and the others couldn't help but join in. Several minutes passed by and their van still had not arrived.

"Maybe they got a flat?" Ryan proposed.

"Yeah, probably so," Tom said. "Let's wait five more minutes and then we can load up and drive down there. I'd hate to miss out on a day of work just because the van has a flat."

"I'm with you on that," Amber said. "We can get two more in our car. Does anyone else have a vehicle."

"Tom and I both do," Bonnie said. "I think we can all get down to the farm without any problem."

At 6:30, the convoy pulled out of the parking lot and headed south toward the farm. Tiny and Giant went with Tom because his truck was the only one big enough to hold Tiny comfortably. Erv went with Michelle and Bonnie, but Michelle made him ride in the back.

The two lane highway took them about twenty miles south and then they turned off on a side road they all recognized because of the falling down plain wood barn that stood at the intersection. A rusty windmill on a wooden frame was west of the barn. Those two things were all that remained of the farm that had once flourished there.

The tar and chip back road ran straight as an arrow. The three vehicles clipped along nicely, remembering to move to the edge when they topped a hill. Bonnie felt a sense of relaxation driving in such a wide open environment. No traffic or stoplights to worry about, she could simply drive. She watched as simple farmhouses drifted by on her left and then a massive hog farm that occupied nearly one hundred acres at the corner where they made the next turn.

After another right, they turned onto the road that led to the farm where they had been working. This road bore little traffic, so the maintenance had been allowed to slip. The drivers were trying to avoid large potholes, so they were going quite a bit slower when they came up out the wooded bottom ground just before the farm.

"Something isn't right," Erv said.

"What do you mean?" Bonnie asked, slowing to turn in.

"I don't know, but I feel it in my bones."

"What the…," Michelle said, leaning forward. She was looking directly out across the spot where the farmhouse had once stood.

"What is it?" Bonnie asked, stopping the car.

"The office trailer is gone," Erv said in disbelief.

Tom gave a quick tap on his horn and drew the attention of those in Bonnie's car. Michelle rolled down her window and looked up at the driver's side window.

"The trailer is gone," Tom said.

"We noticed that, too," Michelle said as she watched Amber direct their car further down the driveway and stop outside the first shed they had worked in. The others got out and started walking that way.

"It's all gone," Ryan said, stepping back out of the shadows of the shed's entrance.

"What do you mean?" Giant asked as he reached the back end of Amber's car.

"The equipment is gone," Ryan said, throwing his hands in the air. "I mean, I didn't check the other shed, but this one is empty."

"Look at the grass," Amber said. "It's all mashed down like a fleet of trucks came through here."

"That's exactly what happened," Michelle said. "It would've taken a couple dozen trucks to haul all of that off in a single day."

"I bet they had the trucks waiting just down the road when they sent us back to the hotel the other day," Erv said. "Look at the path back to the other shed. That grass is flattened, too. They are gone for sure."

"The equipment is gone, just like our pay," Bonnie said. Silence was the only response as everyone stared into the empty shed.

"Did any of you sign a contract?" Ryan asked. "I know we didn't."

"Nope," Giant said. "It was a straight cash deal. That seemed like the best part and now looks to be the worst."

"Gary must have a credit card on file back at the hotel," Michelle said. "I bet he has contact information for the company, too. He seems like a good guy. I bet he'll help us out."

"Then, let's go," Tom said before rushing back to his truck. All three vehicles started up, turned around in the overgrown grass, and headed back for the hotel.

Tom usually kept a calm demeanor, but this had set him off. He led the line of cars at just over eighty miles per hour once they hit the highway. He stopped his truck in the first spot after the handicap reserved space near the motel office entrance. Gary heard them pull up and came out of his little room.

"You all are back early," Gary said with a smile, which faded when he saw the look on Tom's face. He looked at the others and realized something had gone wrong. "What happened? Is everyone okay?"

"The place we were working has been vacated, which means we didn't get paid," Bonnie said. "Will you give us the contact information for whoever paid for our rooms?"

"Sure," Gary said, looking shocked. "I keep all that in my office."

"Did they pay you up front for our rooms?" Michelle asked, causing Gary to freeze. He turned and looked at her.

"No," Gary said. "I keep a card on file and run it when the stay is complete."

"You might want to do that," Michelle said, crossing her arms.

Gary stepped into his office and pulled out the paperwork for their reservation. He typed the card information into his machine and waited. Seconds later, it came back 'Declined'. He tried it again but got the same result. He tore off the little slip and wandered back out to the lobby. Everyone could see the disbelief in his eyes and then anger.

He went right back in and grabbed the whole folder. He brought it back into the lobby and put it on the counter. He flipped to the page with the contact information and put his finger on the phone number. A swipe with his left hand took the receiver cleanly from its cradle, and he dialed the number.

"Six rooms per night for four weeks," Gary murmured. "That's over twelve thousand dollars. Should've known."

"We're sorry. The number you have dialed is not a working number. Please hang up and try the number again," the automated voice on the line said. "We're sorry…"

Gary hung up and stared at his guests. "It looks like we are all in the same boat," he said.

"At least you have a contract," Giant said.

"Sure, but how much is that worth if I can't get ahold of them. It isn't like I have an attorney on retainer, and I can't afford to hire one. I'm about three grand behind on bills and was counting on this to get back in the black."

"That sucks," Erv said.

"Sheesh," Gary said. "I didn't mean to drop all that on you guys. It just sort of came out."

"No worries," Bonnie said. "I guess we'll get our stuff."

"No, that's okay," Gary said after taking a deep breath. "You were all caught off guard by this too and now you probably don't have much cash. You can stay here a couple more days if you want."

"We will throw in what we can," Ryan said from the back of the group.

"Anything would be appreciated," Gary replied and looked down at the folder.

The group retreated to their own rooms to consider the situation but agreed to meet in Bonnie's room at two to come up with a plan.

"So, anyone have a clue what they are going to do?" Erv asked. "I feel like a plastic sack in the wind about now."

"I'm with Erv on that," Michelle said. "I guess I'll head back to Columbia, but living on my dad's couch isn't what I was hoping for."

"Tiny and I talked," Giant said.

"Tiny talked?" Bonnie asked with a smile.

"Yes," Giant said. "He talks quite a bit when it is just the two of us. We have some friends down in the Cherokee nation. They will hopefully put us up for the winter and we'll work off whatever we use. Not a money maker, but we have to survive. The only thing we don't like about the situation is that it is unlikely they can support all eight of us."

"Don't worry about that," Bonnie said. "It has been great working together, but finding work for all of us in one spot won't happen. Finding a job for one or two is hard enough. How are you going to get down there?"

"Same as always," Giant said. "We'll hitch and walk. If we're lucky, we'll catch some literary nut that equates us to George and Lenny. We made it from Sacramento to Salt Lake City once with a college professor who talked Steinbeck the whole way. Tiny had to explain most of it to me once we got to Utah."

"Ryan and I are probably going north. Maybe Omaha," Amber said. "I have a cousin up there who does property management. We are hoping she can use a couple maintenance workers."

"Worth a shot," Erv said. "How about you, Tom?"

"I still have my little apartment in St. Louis," Tom said. "I guess I'll go back up there and see what I can figure out. The place is small, but I can fit one person on the sofa."

"I'm going to hang out here," Bonnie said. "Gary is willing to put us up while I figure things out, so I'm going to see if I can help him out a little and then hope for the best on finding a destination."

"You don't want to come back to St. Louis?" Tom asked with obvious disappointment.

"I don't think so. I need something different. I want to make a difference, so maybe I'll go to Springfield or Joplin and try to find a charity to work for."

"That sounds noble," Michelle said. "Sounds like you might get hungry pretty fast."

"Could be," Bonnie said, shrugging. "It might not work, but I have to try."

"I applaud that mindset," Michelle said. "Let's all exchange phone numbers so we can be in touch if someone stumbles on a great opportunity."

"That works for me," Erv said. "If Bonnie isn't going to St. Louis, can I join you, Tom? I really don't have anywhere to go, and a sofa sounds a whole lot better than any alternative I can see."

"You got it," Tom said. He patted Erv on the shoulder. They each wrote down their contact information and traded.

Amber and Ryan left that afternoon. Tiny and Giant were off the next morning. Tom and Erv dropped them off at a truck stop along Interstate 44, saving them that much of a walk. Michelle took a ride from Bonnie to get to the bus station in Springfield and bought a ticket to Columbia with what she had left. At the end of that painful day, Bonnie returned to her room at Motel 5 and stared at the ceiling until she fell asleep.

6

"Good morning, Bonnie," Gary said when walked into the lobby two mornings later. "Not much on the breakfast menu this morning. You are the only one here, sorry."

"Don't be," Bonnie said. "I wish you had a hotel full of paying guests."

"Then you'll be happy to hear that I've got seventy-five rooms rented starting next Monday," Gary said. "Apparently there is a big construction job coming into the area and they need a place for everyone to stay. And, yes, I got a deposit this time. They didn't even question why I would want one, just put up twenty-five grand and told me to let them know when that was used up."

"Good for you, Gary! Why don't you let me help you out with freshening up the rooms? It is the least I can do."

"I'll pay you for that."

"Up to you, but I think the free room and board warrants a couple days of work."

"That wasn't your fault," Gary said. "I guess you are planning on heading out soon?"

"You generously offered a few more days and that time is up."

"I'll still have a couple extra rooms if you want to stay. I shouldn't have put a time limit on you. It was a bad day."

"For all of us," Bonnie said, smiling at her host. "I'm thinking about going over to Joplin and seeing what pops up. I've heard they have some openings at a factory over there for minimum wage."

"Well, if that doesn't work out, come on back this way."

"I did think of a way to make some money though," Bonnie said, smiling again. "I'm going to go back down to the farm where we were working and see if they left behind any tools or supplies that might be worth something. I figure a little theft from an abandoned place like that won't draw much attention."

"Was there anything good down there?"

"They had several pressure washers, some basic tools, ladders, and so on."

"I could use a pressure washer," Gary said. "I tell you what, why don't you take my panel van down there and load it with whatever you can get. If you get a pressure washer, I'll buy it from you. I'm all for sticking it to those people."

"Me too," she said. "I'll trade you the pressure washer for the use of the van."

"That's a better deal for me than you."

"I'm okay with it. I'm going to grab some cereal and head south."

"Okay," Gary said, reaching under the counter and producing a set of keys. "Happy hunting!"

After a bowl of Cheerios and two cups of coffee, Bonnie was on her way. She had to adjust to riding much higher than she did in her car, but she enjoyed the change in perspective. She followed the normal route but had to stop when she got ready to make her second turn.

One of the long, brown hog barns was on fire. A stream of animals was rushing away from the burning building. They had poured across the narrow strip of ground between the barn and the road but pooled there, as the pasture on the other side of the road had a wooden fence along its border. The hogs swarmed but could only move in a confused manner along the pavement. She could see several men rushing around, trying to hose down the building, and she did not envy their work in rounding up the escaped animals.

Instead of turning, she continued straight, hoping to find a different road that would take her to the farm. It took an extra thirty minutes, but she found her way. It was on her left as she approached, instead of her right.

"Way to go, Bonnie," she said to herself as she parked in front of the nearest big shed. "Now let's see what kind of treasures we can turn up."

Four ladders, a wheelbarrow, and two pressure washers were the first things in the van. She was glad Gary had loaned her his ride. She used a pry bar she found to break the lock off of a closet in the second shed and found a rolling tool chest. It was too heavy for her to pick up, but she pulled out each drawer and set it in the van. The chest would have brought good money. The tools were in good shape, and she was sure they would buy her a month of food.

Within an hour, she had loaded up everything that she could find that was worth selling. She was about to call it a day when she glanced around and had a new thought. One of the drawers had been full of a variety of pliers, so she found a nice pair of side cutters. She pulled the main breaker from the panel and started cutting out all the copper wire she could reach. She would talk to Gary about metal recyclers in the area that wouldn't ask too many questions.

The sun was well past midday when she decided to move along. The cereal had long since served its purpose and she needed to find something to eat. She was about to start the van when her eyes settled on the grain bins on the far side of the clearing. She wondered if there was anything in them and could she sell that if there was.

Minutes later, she used a block of wood to hammer on the side of the first bin and was rewarded with a dull thud. It was far from empty, and the second bin had the same sound. It would take two or three semis to haul it all off and she only had a van. She was debating what to do and thought of a trailer she had seen in the weeds behind the second shed.

Luck was with her as the ball hitch on Gary's van fit the trailer, which was actually an old orange truck bed that had been modified with a tongue. She spent an hour scooping grain from the pile that poured out the door on the side of the first bin. The trailer was full, but she was worried that the old tires wouldn't hold up to that much weight. They held for as long as she needed them to, though.

The van was hauling a load that taxed its very being. Bonnie recognized that and crept along the backroads, never breaking twenty miles an hour. She was focused so much on getting back to town that she forgot about the pigs and their roadblock. So, a short while later she stopped and stared at what looked to be at least two hundred hogs still blocking the roadway.

The fire dwindled. Only a thin twist of smoke was rising from the far end of the building. A man in muddied work boots and carrying a shovel walked over to the side of the van. He was grinning and gave a friendly wave, so Bonnie rolled down her window.

"Sorry about our little mess," he said. "We had to let them out when the barn caught on fire but didn't anticipate they would go this way."

"No problem," she said, looking back at the pigs. "I was by here earlier and should have known to take a different route. Now I've got a load on, and I don't know which way to go with this corn."

"If you don't mind me asking, where did you get it? Most people haul corn in a semi, not a rusted out converted truck bed."

"Long story, but I got screwed over by some people who were cleaning out a farm back that way."

"Oh, probably the Elwood farm," he said, nodding. "A hush hush deal that none of us really know much about."

"Well, we did a ton of work for them getting equipment ready to sell and then they skipped out on us. Took the equipment but didn't pay us a dime."

"So, you took their corn?"

"Seems fair to me."

"Oh, absolutely," he said. "Looks like you got several other things in your van."

"Doing my best to take advantage of the situation."

"Good for you. What are you going to do with that corn?"

"I don't know exactly. I'm hoping to find an elevator or something. I looked it up and prices are around three twenty-five a bushel."

"Impressive." he said. "You did your homework. The problem is that the nearest elevator is about seventy miles from here. Most farmers haul their grain all the way to the railroad now to keep some extra bucks."

"That sucks for me, then."

"Maybe not, hold on," he said and walked back toward a small office building. He waved to an older man who looked exhausted, having just walked away from where the fire had been. The man talked with his hands, pointing at the trailer and then back toward the farm. The older man was listening while tapping his shovel on the ground. Then, without saying a word to the younger man, he walked over to the van.

"Afternoon, young lady," he said, when he reached the fence. "Adam, here, tells me you've got some corn to sell. Oh, excuse my lack of manners, I'm Louis Kent and I manage this farm."

"I'm Bonnie Rose," she said, rolling down the window the rest of the way. "Yes, I do have some corn to sell."

"I'd say there is about fifty bushel in there," Louis said, gesturing to the trailer. "I'm surprised that old trailer's axle didn't break with that much weight."

"Fifty bushels?" Bonnie wondered. "At three twenty per bushel is... around a hundred and sixty bucks."

She looked ahead of her at the hogs and thought about the fact that she could maybe get two nights in a hotel for that money. Louis cleared his throat, drawing her attention back to the conversation.

"Yep, that's the price if you deliver it all the way to the railroad. You are a long way from the railroad. Perhaps we can work a deal," Louis said, looking over to Adam. Adam had walked back to the trailer and started inspecting the corn. Bonnie was watching him in the side mirror. "As you can imagine, I use quite a bit of corn in my feed mixture for all these hogs. So, how about I buy your trailer full of corn for a hundred even."

"And the rest of it?"

"Back at the other farm? I can't risk getting caught taking it. That'd be theft and I'd lose my job."

"Look, I'm all about abiding by the rules, but these people really hurt my friends and me. I want to make them suffer. They weren't smart enough to haul the grain off when they took the equipment. I'll lease a semi, if I have to."

"I like your grit," Louis said. "I tell you what, I'll send a couple guys over tomorrow morning with a couple semis and see how much we can get. There isn't a farm place for miles anymore, so we might do okay."

"That's a lot of corn for you. How does it help me?"

Louis could not stop the smile from spreading across his face.

"I'll supply the trucks, the manpower, the tractor, and the auger you'd need to unload those bins in any sort of a reasonable time frame. I'll pay you a dollar a bushel for everything we get."

"Forgive me, but I don't have the highest level of trust for strangers promising me money in the future."

"I understand," Louis said, looking serious. "I've got four thousand hogs here and there is no way I could move them all away before tomorrow. I'm just hoping Adam and the boys can get them back in the barn tonight."

Louis could see she wasn't convinced.

"Where are you staying?"

"What?"

"I'm only asking because I know pretty much everyone in town, and they can vouch for me. Harry Jones at the auto parts shop. Martha Rateliff at Martha's guns and liquor, she's quite a character. Gary Floyd at Motel 5, maybe?"

"I know who Gary is," she said.

"Ah, right," Louis said. "I should have been paying attention. That's Gary's van, I think. Let me call him right quick."

"No," Bonnie said. "That's not necessary. If you recognize the van, then I'm good. Besides, you are going to give me two hundred in cash before I leave."

"Well, now," Louis said. "I like the way you work. Once we have the grain loaded up, we can settle up the difference."

"I think we have a deal."

She went back to the motel and showed Gary everything she had found at the farm. She thought about the cash in her pocket and told him she had made a deal on some of what she had found. In exchange for two more nights at the motel, she gave him everything that was in the van. Gary was ecstatic.

7

Bonnie had breakfast at the roadhouse the next morning. Steak, eggs, biscuits, bacon, and pancakes got her started. The waitress didn't seem to think someone her size could handle that much food, but Bonnie obliterated it. It felt good to be that full. She thought she might go back to the motel for a morning nap but went for a drive instead.

A two-lane highway carried her west out of town and into the middle of nowhere. She loved it. The peaceful countryside made her relax. She stopped at a little rest area that was really nothing more than a pair of brown outhouses and four green picnic tables. A single water faucet with a drinking fountain attached to the side stuck out of a concrete slab between the two little shacks. A half dozen pine trees made a sort of half circle barrier around the back of the area.

It was November in Southwest Missouri, but the day was fantastic. The display on her car said it was sixty-two outside with clouds spotting the blue sky. Bonnie surprised herself when her stomach growled just before one. A little bulletin board with a roof stood to the left of the outhouses. Bonnie discovered that there was a gas station with a diner about five miles ahead and that she was near Wilson's Creek, a civil war battlefield and park. She had always enjoyed history, so she got lunch and then went to explore the park.

Alice's Restaurant was a small, rectangular building with green siding and a black shingled roof that was well past needing to be replaced. Five glass windows made up most of the front of the place with a single glass door at the far east end. Bonnie left the highway in favor of the crushed gravel parking lot in front of Alice's, there were only two other cars. She assumed those belonged to the workers.

"Welcome to Alice's Restaurant," a woman in her early forties said as soon as Bonnie was through the door. Her fiery red hair had streaks of silver and was pulled back into a ponytail. She was chomping away on a piece of gum and looked generally uninterested in what she was doing. "I'm Alice. You want a drink?"

"Sure," Bonnie said, taking a seat at the counter. The scene was fascinating, and she felt like she had fallen into a movie. "Coke or Pepsi?"

"We got both, honey."

"Pepsi, then. Thanks."

"Sure thing," Alice said and walked off toward the cooler at the far end of the counter. She had a slight limp and held onto the edge of the bar on her way down and back.

"Know what you want to eat?" Alice asked, placing a glass bottle of Pepsi on the counter in front of Bonnie. She wasn't sure when she had last seen a glass bottle of soda.

"I had a big breakfast," Bonnie said, looking down at her menu. "Is the full menu available?"

"You can get anything you want at Alice's Restaurant," Alice said, although the phrase was lost on Bonnie who had never heard of Arlo Guthrie.

"How about…"

"Go with the bacon double cheese and house seasoned fries," said a woman to Alice's right. "Mel does it all well, but those are to die for."

"I didn't hear you come in, Alicia," Alice said. "Yeah, Mel makes a good burger. I've had too many in my time."

"I'll take that, then," Bonnie said and stuck the menu back in the little silver stand next to the napkin dispenser.

"It'll be out shortly," Alice said and walked away. "Hey, Alicia, take care of her. I'm going to make a call."

"Okay, Mom."

"Alice and Alicia, huh," Bonnie said, looking at Alicia, who appeared younger than her. She had the same red hair as her mom, but it was curly and short.

"Yep, just glad not to be another Alice," she said. "My grandma was the original Alice, and she named her daughter Alice, but I lucked out. Mel is my uncle, but my mom owns the place. I guess I'll inherit it someday if I'm lucky."

Alicia had a playful smile on her face and Bonnie could tell she was trying not to laugh. She straightened the little paper hat she was wearing and tied on an apron.

"So, what brings you out this way? We don't do a great business anymore."

"Sorry to hear that. I guess it's kind of going around," Bonnie said. "I saw a sign for Wilson's Creek Battlefield and thought I'd check it out."

"Well, hopefully you didn't drive too far. When the feds cut the funding for the Park Service, Wilson's Creek was one of the first to go. I guess they figured it was too far out from the almighty interstate and people wouldn't miss it."

"That sucks."

"Yeah, especially since ninety percent of our business came from visitors to the park."

"Just between you and me, I'm not easily deterred. I'll probably go in anyway and have a look around. I bet it is beautiful this time of year."

"Oh, it certainly is. The creeks are crystal clear, and the last of the colors on the trees are magnificent," Alicia said. "The thing is that they cut all the staff, but they put up security cameras along the road leading into the park. One guy took down the chain across the road and went in about a month ago, but the sheriff was there before he could get past Wilson's cabin."

"Pretty protective of a place they aren't using."

"Yeah, word is that the sheriff's department is getting a paycheck to keep a close eye on it. Keeps the Park Service from having any employees out there. Such a joke."

"I guess that means I'll be hiking in from the main road," Bonnie said.

"Order up!" Mel called from the passthrough window.

Alicia made a quick round trip, placing one of the juiciest cheeseburgers with the freshest toppings that Bonnie had ever seen on the counter in front of her. She also left two folded paper napkins and another one wrapped around the silverware.

"Not saying you'll make a mess, but Mel's burgers are dripping with goodness," Alicia said.

"No offense taken!" Bonnie said, debating where to start on the burger.

"Let me know if you need anything," Alicia said before walking away.

Bonnie had been about to ask her another question about the park, but it was lost in the deliciousness on a platter. The fries were crispy, but not burned. The burger had cheddar and Swiss cheeses, crunchy bacon, and patties that were full of flavor. Not to mention the thick slice of tomato, onions, and lettuce. Bonnie thought of nothing else for the next twenty minutes.

"Leave any room for dessert?" Alicia asked.

Bonnie slid the napkin across her mouth. A faraway look was in her eyes, and she sighed with satisfaction. Finally, she looked up at Alicia and smiled.

"I think I will literally explode if I eat anything else."

"We have the best shakes in the state. Hand dipped with real fruit if you want."

"Ugh. Yes, I want one," Bonnie said. "I'm going to have to wait though. If I drink a shake, I won't be able to make the walk back into the park."

"I tell you what. You promise to come back in for a shake later on and I'll give you a little tip that will save you a bunch of steps."

"I can't refuse that!"

"Alright," Alicia said, looking around as if someone might be eavesdropping. "If you go about a quarter of a mile past the entrance to the park, you'll see a field road. It should be nice and dry, so your car will handle it. That road runs right along the edge of the park property, and you'll see a small grove of trees where the field road turns west. There is a little clearing in those trees where you can park your car and it won't be seen from the main road. High school and college kids may or may not use that as a spot to, well, you know."

"I'm guessing it won't be in use during broad daylight?"

"Probably not, but it really depends on the day. Lock your doors. Anyway, you'll only be about a hundred yards from Wilson's Cabin at that point. It is supposed to be the home of the guy the park is named after, but it's modern. It was used as the information center. The cameras are only on the driveway, so you can get back into the park easily from there."

"That's awesome," Bonnie said. "I'll be back for at least one milkshake, then."

"Glad we could do business," Alicia said.

"Keep the change," Bonnie said, placing a twenty on the counter. "I'll see you later."

"Thank you very much!"

Bonnie went to her car and headed west along the two lane highway. She saw the entrance to the park and the signs warning people not to trespass. The field road that Alicia had talked about was exactly one quarter of a mile past the chained entrance to Wilson's Creek.

Her car bounced a little on the ruts, but the ground was hard. She had no problem getting from the highway to the grove of trees. The trees stood bare, having already dropped their leaves for the season, but the undergrowth was thick. It took a few minutes for her to find the flattened down weeds at the west end, but then she drove easily back between the trees.

When she got out, she smiled. The weeds were tall enough to hide her car and there was no dust drifting from the field road to tip people off that she had come back here.

She pulled a gray hooded sweatshirt with a Cardinals logo from the back seat. She zipped it up three quarters of the way and grabbed a bottle of water from the console between the front seats.

The breeze had a cooler touch once she was in the trees, but it felt good. As she made her way along the faint path, the cheeseburger settled in her stomach and a nap was irresistible. The walking helped her stay awake. The path disappeared a couple times, but she was able to pick her way through the mix of trees on the west edge of the park. Finally, she emerged onto a gravel path and turned left toward the cabin.

Bonnie thought the small cabin looked to be built from oversized Lincoln Logs, like the ones she had played with as a kid. If the building had worn a green plastic roof, it would have been perfect. After looking around, she decided that there was no reason to be concerned at this point. A large map of the entire park was mounted to the side of the cabin under a piece of plexiglass. She was surprised to see how big the park actually was and thought it might take a couple days to explore it all.

The rock path she had been on was labeled as the Green Trail. It went back past where she had left her car and then wound into the edge of the Ozark Mountains. A campground was notated near one of the branches of Wilson's Creek and she thought it would be a good target for that day.

The park had not been closed long enough to allow things to fall into disrepair, so Bonnie had a nice hike. She followed a trail that gradually took her up a rise and then back down a switchback path that led to the campground situated at the edge of the creek. Eight wood sided houses that were half the size of the main cabin stood in a line. She peeked in one window and saw a cozy little scene.

The kitchenette with black appliances and oak cabinets was to the left of the front door. A wooden table stained in a dark tone with four matching chairs was directly below the window she was looking in and a queen bed with a blue and yellow striped comforter stood in the corner to her right. At the far right corner of the room was a pair of plush, blue couches that looked like a perfect nap location. A little room was built into the corner next to the bed. She assumed that had to be the bathroom.

This sort of camping wasn't as challenging as what her foster dad had told her about from when he was a kid in the Boy Scouts.

The golden orange of the setting sun was beginning to fade, and she glanced at her watch. She thought it should still be a while until sunset but started back anyway. While surveying the camping area, she noticed that a dirt path ran west, meandering with the creek branch. She guessed that she was within a hundred yards of the edge of the park and went to see if she could get to her car that way.

The dirt path was a little harder to negotiate, but she enjoyed the sound of the branches as she walked. The rise she had come down was on her right and the slope of the creek rose to meet it as she neared the edge of the park. The creek made a sharp turn to the south, and she saw that the trees ended just a little bit ahead of her.

Bonnie left the dirt path and walked out into the bright sunshine. She was amazed at how much the trees blocked the light. A field road that looked similar to the one she had driven on earlier ran along the trees. She looked out across the field and saw that it ran north, then west to the edge of a large patch of trees, and then north again.

The little grove where she had left her car stood across the field that was covered with cut-off corn stalks. She realized that if she drove further down the field road, she could get close to the campground. There was no way she would be spotted back here. She would return the next day and start her hike from the campground.

8

Bonnie woke up feeling sore. She knew it had been a long time since she had taken that long of a hike. Her legs and back felt like they were on fire. She dug out her bottle of aspirin and took three pills. A quick shower was next and then she started toward the lobby. The weather was beautiful. She wondered if she could make it back out to the park that day. The calf on her left leg cramped, as if it knew what she was thinking.

Once she got to the lobby, she sat down to rub her sore leg. Gary was sitting behind the counter on his familiar stool sipping a cup of coffee and staring at the morning paper. He did not greet her.

"Hey, Gary," she said, continuing to massage her leg.

"Oh, hey Bonnie. Sorry, I guess I was zoned out."

"Everything okay? You seem off this morning."

"Got some bad news this morning. Bittersweet, I guess."

"Did that big rental back out?"

"Just the opposite, actually," he said, folding up his paper. "They secured all my rooms for ten months."

"That's awesome!" Bonnie said.

"Yeah, but Charlie from over at the post office stopped by to tell me what they were here to build."

"And?"

"Apparently some big development firm out of Tulsa chose our little interstate exchange as the perfect spot for their next project. The guys staying here will be building two hotels, four restaurants, and preparing several other building sites. Charlie said they are likely putting in a Wal-Mart. It's going to kill Motel 5 and most of the other local places."

"Wow, that's awful."

"You know," Gary said, "I shouldn't even be complaining. Especially not to you. I've got a really good income for the next year. Do you even know where you are going tomorrow? I can still make a room available if you need it."

"Nope, don't worry. I've got some cash, and my car is hitting on all cylinders. I'll be okay. Besides, you need to squeeze every dollar you can out of these guys."

"Well, if you are in the area, stop in and say hello. I think I'll be pretty bored with no change in guests. They agreed to only having the rooms made up once per week, so I won't be busy."

"Good for you," she said. "Mind if I get some breakfast?"

"Go for it," he said. "I made some eggs and picked up some bagels at Beth's Bakery. They are pretty good. Actually, they are the best I've ever had."

"Thanks, Gary. Are you a big bagel fan, then?"

"No, not really. I like my doughnuts," he said with a sheepish grin.

"Nothing wrong with a good doughnut."

Bonnie spent the day relaxing on her bed, watching random movies. It felt good to do nothing, but searching the park stayed at the front of her mind. The milkshake she had gotten from Alicia kept breaking into her other thoughts. She planned on having another very soon.

By the time Bonnie had put everything in her car the next morning, seven white pickups and two utility vans had arrived at Motel 5. Her car slipped out of the parking lot unnoticed by anyone, except Gary. He was sitting on his stool watching the men mill about outside, thinking about the future.

Bonnie had a plan and it started at Jentsen's grocery store. She bought peanut butter, bread, bottled water, cereal, and several other things she thought would get her through the next week. Then, she went west along the familiar two lane highway that led to Wilson's Creek. The campground was her destination.

She cruised past Alice's diner, thinking she would have to splurge at least once in the next week for one of those burgers and another shake. Then again, she had a craving for strawberries that morning. Maybe she'd get a strawberry milkshake with a Belgian waffle the next time. A smirk crept across her face when she passed the chained entrance to Wilson's Creek. The field road was waiting for her, but she took a moment to make sure no one was coming along the highway. There was a clear view for at least a mile in either direction, so she wanted to be positive no one was coming.

Bonnie turned to where she had hidden her car days earlier and continued away from the highway. When she got to the furthest west part of the field road, she realized the area next to the timber ground was rougher than the rest of the road. She crept along, trying to avoid the bigger ruts, but stopped when she noticed a half dozen hogs creeping up out of the trees.

They stopped at a low wooden fence that was about three feet inside the tree line. Several more joined them when she got out. She returned their gaze. Bonnie was intrigued by how different this style of hog farming was from what she had seen before. There was no barn in sight, let alone a farm. Out of nowhere, she had a sudden feeling of confidence and energy. The pain in her leg went away, as if she had gotten a shot of adrenaline.

Five minutes later she found a spot along the field road where she could park her car. It was not visible from the main road and would be hard to see even from the hog timber thanks to a slight dip in the terrain.

Bonnie clipped the four grocery bags to her backpack using a pair of carabiners and started into the trees. The walk out felt much longer, so she was pleased to realize the first cabin was only about ten minutes from her car. She attributed that to going downhill and familiarity with her destination.

She crossed her fingers and turned the knob on the first cabin. It held firm and she figured all the cabins would be the same, but she wanted to try. The second and third cabin yielded the same result, but the doorknob turned on the fourth and she gave a short laugh of excitement. A bird fluttered away from the eave above her, startling her and causing her to let go of the doorknob.

She grasped it again and turned, thinking it would probably be locked this time. It wasn't, so she pushed. The door did not budge, so she pushed a little harder. She wondered if the door or frame had expanded a little in the fall weather. A moment later it gave a little, but she realized it was sticking at the top of the door. When she looked up, she saw that there was a deadbolt lock up there and cursed her bad luck. In her frustration, she gave two more solid shoves and heard the wooden frame creak.

"Come on, Muscles," she said, repeating a line her foster dad had used years before when encouraging her to try harder.

She braced herself with a powerful stance and leaned into the door while turning the knob. She heard another creak but was about to give it up and try the next cabin. Then, that wave of confidence she had felt near the hog timber came back and she pushed harder. The door protested and that drew more power from her legs. Finally, the frame gave a loud crack, and the door flew open.

Bonnie grabbed the frame and stopped her forward momentum, keeping her from falling on her face. A chunk of the frame was lying on the floor halfway across the room near the foot of the queen sized bed.

"Nicely done," she said, feeling proud. The cabin looked better from the inside than what she had thought from her earlier observation. She put her groceries in the kitchenette area, her backpack on the table next to the bed, and gave three solid pushes on the mattress. It was softer than the one at Motel 5.

Although the door had been deadbolted, all the utilities were still on. She guessed the water came from a well and thought maybe they left the utilities on hoping that the park would reopen soon. Hot water ran from the tap in the kitchen, thanks to an electric water heater, and the light in the refrigerator came on when she opened the door. This cabin was going to work out much better than she had hoped.

She had an early lunch of peanut butter with a sliced up Granny Smith apple. Then, she went east along the branch. The rock path was in great shape as she went deeper into the park. The relaxing sound of a light wind through the treetops and the babble of the branch made her forget her worries. The equipment cleaning, the vacated grocery warehouse in Saint Louis, and even concerns over being spotted in the park were gone.

The next four days were some of the best she could remember. The east boundary of the park was similar to the west but provided a great view of the sunrise on the second day. The south boundary was much harder to get to and required her to do some climbing on the morning of the fourth day.

The southern path curved east and then went back north, but she wanted to see the whole park. Moss and thin weeds covered most of the rock face, but she found a narrow section that was bare. As she looked up, she thought about how hard those fifteen or twenty feet would be.

"You got this," she said, bringing that new confidence back.

Her fingers gripped the rocks with ease, and she started up. The shoes were not meant for climbing and the left one lost its hold about halfway up. She thought she was going to fall, but her fingers held tight. Bonnie had always considered her legs to be strong, but her grip had never been anything to brag about.

She made it to the top of the ledge and ventured south until she found the park's border. When she sat on top of a dried out old stump, she felt accomplished. The land to the south was not being farmed, so the wild grasses provided a beautiful scene. The tips of grass moved in great waves as if she was looking out at a yellow lake. After enjoying the view for a while, she went out to stand in the grass and feel it brush against her. The tips gently touching her palms were relaxing. She stood there for a while, unconcerned with how much time had passed.

A little while later, hunger interrupted her thoughts as she stared into nature. There was a granola bar in her backpack, but she felt like she could eat one of Mel's cheeseburgers plus a milkshake. A glance to her right revealed a white plastic pole marking the corner of the park a short distance away. The grass looked like it would be easy to walk through and then she could walk north to her car. A trip to Alice's was in order.

The thought of getting the burger brought a strong wave of hunger, and she had the granola bar while she walked. It did not take long to go around the edge of the park. Her car was waiting for her, and she was relieved to see no one had tried to break in. She unlocked the driver side door, slid in, and put the key in the ignition. Normally, she would have heard a repeated dinging, but it wasn't there. She gave the key a twist and nothing happened.

Bonnie tried a couple more times before leaning back in her seat and staring at the dash. She knew that the lights in the display should be on, even if the battery was almost dead. There was nothing, so she popped the hood and went to look. The sight that greeted her was hard to believe. There was a field rat the size of her fist on top of the battery. Its eyes were bulging and the fur around its mouth was scorched. The little beast had fried itself while chewing on the battery lead.

The sun was drifting down toward the hog timber, and she thought it might be time to go back to the cabin. She could get something to eat and think of a way to fix this. However, the burger was calling to her and she thought it would be nice to actually talk to someone. Alicia would be a good choice to serve as that outlet, so she put on her backpack and started toward the highway. That mistake would lead to a big change in her life.

The field road ran straight along the edge of the trees, and she was enjoying the view. She wondered if Alicia would be working. Her plan hadn't accounted for other waitresses, not even Alice.

Bonnie looked ahead and then to her right. That's when she saw a plain white Chevy sedan backed in between the trees. It looked like a police car, and fear rushed over her. She could not see anyone with the car, so she hurried on. Ducking into the trees once she got a little further felt like the best plan. When she was past the car, she heard a metallic click.

"Stop there," said a man's deep voice. Bonnie froze. "Turn around."

She turned to see a man in a flannel shirt and jeans. His shaggy brown hair was sticking out from under a filthy seed cap. He was smiling, pointing a pistol at her.

"Are you a cop?"

"Huh? Oh, the car. I bought that at the surplus sale last year. My sister's ex is the sheriff though. We are still friends. I bet he'd love to know another one of you hippies was out here in the park again."

"I was just walking."

"Well, now you are done walking. It's time for you to go for a ride. I guess we will have to see how much you want to stay out of trouble."

Bonnie's stomach turned as she stared at the man's evil grin. His teeth were a mix of yellow and brown with four missing on the left side of his mouth. He gestured toward the car with the gun. She thought he would probably use the gun if she didn't cooperate. Getting into this car could be the death of her, and she wished for help.

"Open the back door and get in," he said, the smile gone.

"Please don't hurt me," she said, sitting down on the back bench seat.

"That's up to you," he said and tossed two pairs of handcuffs on her lap. "Put one set on your ankles and one on your wrists. I can't risk you jumping out of the car or making a run for it."

She stared at the silver cuffs.

"Do it," he said. Finally, she put the cuffs around her ankles and winced when they clicked shut. The feeling of the cold metal around her wrists did not make her feel any better. "Good. Now, let's go."

He slammed her door. Bonnie watched him walk around the car to slide into the driver's seat. He tossed his cap into the passenger seat, and she saw that he was completely bald. She thought he looked to be in his thirties, so the cap was surely his way of hiding his smooth head.

The car bumped a little as it pulled out onto the field road. They weren't far from the first bend and were soon headed west toward the hog timber. Bonnie looked toward the highway, wishing that someone would come along and see them. She wasn't sure anyone would do anything, but she had to hope.

The car turned with the road and slowed. The holes that Bonnie's car had struggled with were not any easier for this sedan. She looked out into the timber and saw a pig staring back at her, as if it were trying to speak to her. She sighed and the pig turned away.

"Hold on back there," the man said, trying to avoid the bigger holes, but still bouncing along. "What the…"

Bonnie looked through the windshield to see eight hogs rush toward the little wooden fence and bust through.

They looked dazed and stood in the middle of the road. The man swerved to his right, trying to avoid them but went into one of the bigger ruts. The front right tire hit the far edge of the rut and gave a great heave. There was a mighty popping sound and the pigs scattered.

"Damn," he said. "I think that was a tire. You stay put."

Bonnie nodded but refused to speak to him. He pulled the lever to release the trunk and got out. She could hear him grumbling as he went to the back of the car and started rearranging things. He went by her window with the spare on the first trip and then with the jack on the second. She looked back toward the timber again and saw the first hog. It was looking at her in that strange way. She wanted to turn away but couldn't. Her door flew open, bringing her back into the moment. He was sweating and looked angry.

"Get out," he said. "I'm going to have to jack this thing and the ground keeps crumbling. You probably weigh a hundred pounds soaking wet, but any relief will help. Now, move."

Bonnie swung her legs out of the door and tried to stand, but that was impossible with the cuffs on and the uneven ground. The man grabbed her by the right wrist and pulled her to her feet. The cuffs cut into her arm, and she winced but refused to let him hear her pain. She could feel his heartbeat pulsing in his strong hand and looked back toward where her car was hidden.

"Don't do anything stupid," he said and walked back toward the flat tire. He put the tire iron on the first lug nut and pushed, finally breaking it loose after stomping on the tool twice. His back was toward her, and she could only watch him, hoping for inspiration of how to get out of this.

"Kill him," said a deep and distant voice. Bonnie was struck dumb for a minute. "He cannot stop us."

Bonnie was confused and did not know what to think about what she was hearing. Surely it was the stress of the situation. This guy was three times her size and certainly could fight back against anything she tried.

"Surprise him. Kill him. He deserves it. He has done this to five other women," the voice said.

"How…," she said.

"What?" the man said, looking back over his shoulder.

"Nothing," Bonnie said. "I was just thinking out loud."

"Don't think too much," he said. "It won't be good for you."

"Okay," she said and looked back at the timber. That same pig was still staring at her.

"Let us in," she heard.

"Okay," she said. A sudden jolt of confidence and confusion overwhelmed her. She wasn't sure what was happening. There was a rumbling in her mind, and she turned back to look at the man's head from behind.

Killing him was not something she would have ever considered, but now it seemed like a viable option. He was grunting as he tried to loosen the fourth lug. Bonnie felt her feet move forward, but it was like they were moving on their own. Her feet shuffled on the dry road. He was too focused on the tire to hear her.

In one swift movement, she put her hands over his head and down onto his shoulders. The short chain linking her wrists stopped at his neck and he stopped moving.

"I told you not to do anything stupid," he said, starting to stand. She pulled her hands back and felt the chain sink into his throat. He grabbed at her hands and tried to get them off his neck. Somehow, she was stronger than him and continued pulling back. He fell over backward, trying to get his breath.

He stood and spun around, but she went with him. Instead, she planted her feet on the side of the car and gave a quick push. This sent them spinning further than he had intended. He went tumbling back down to the dusty ground. Bonnie somehow kept her feet, hopping up his back and over his head. When she did that his head slipped out from between her arms. She spun and took four quick shuffle steps back toward the field. She got into a half crouched position and watched him struggle to get back up.

"You sure are a feisty one," he said, finally gaining his feet and rubbing his neck. He spit dust out of his mouth.

"I'm not sure that is the right word for me," she said.

"Well, you fight pretty good for being so little. What's your name?"

"I am Bon... I am..."

"Cat got your tongue? It doesn't matter anyway. I got my breath back now," he said and rushed toward her. She did not move until he was half a step away and then hopped to her left. He reached out for her, but barely got a fingertip on her left arm before his momentum carried him by. He stumbled on a rut and fell down, striking his head on the hard dirt.

"I am...," she said again, but using her name felt incorrect. She couldn't produce the name Bonnie.

"You know," he said, sitting up, "I was just going to take you back to my place and make you dinner. No funny stuff."

"The handcuffs would lead me to believe you are something less than a gentleman."

He wiped his hand across his cheek, where a rock had given him a cut. The blood was trickling down the side of his face. When he saw the blood on the back of his hand, he looked back at her. A deep furrow formed between his eyes and the corners of his mouth turned down. She watched him ball up his right fist.

"We are...," she said, not knowing why.

"We are what? Going to have some fun tonight? Yeah, one of us is," he said and stood up again.

"We are Legion," she said.

The strength and confidence from earlier pulsed through her again. She pulled her hands apart, and the cuffs began to stretch. The man could have rushed her to maintain control of the situation, but he could not believe what he was seeing. The cuffs pressed into her skin, although she felt no pain. Then, in one fluid motion, she pulled her arms apart and the chain between the cuffs snapped. The weakest of the links spread open and dinged off the side of the car as it flew away. Bonnie flexed her hands as if she were squeezing a stress ball.

"What the…," he said, still staring. "How did you do that?"

A teeth-baring smile stretched across her face while her eyes grew wide. Bonnie felt a sense of joy. She also realized that she had never smiled like that before. Her right leg came up, as if she were stepping out of a pair of jeans that had gathered around her feet. The cuffs grew taut and then snapped with ease. He took a step back but pulled a gun from a holster tucked in the back waistband of his jeans.

"You are crazy strong and that's freaking me out, but I doubt even the strongest person can survive multiple gunshot wounds. One less hippie to worry about. Those pigs will probably enjoy the snack."

Bonnie stood still, staring at him with that same strange grin. He leveled the gun at her and closed his left eye. As his finger slipped into the trigger guard, a deep squeal came from the rear of the car. A large boar raced across the dusty road and the man turned to see it coming, but he was too slow.

The beast plowed into his knees, creating a horrible snapping sound when his leg broke. As he tipped sideways over the massive hog, his hand rose into the air and the gun discharged before flying into the field. The crack of the gun echoed off the wall of trees at the west edge of the park and came back.

Three hours later, a state police cruiser pulled up to the white sedan, but it was no longer on the dusty field road. Now, it sat in the little rest area east of Alice's. Red letters were written across the hood of the car, which is why a passerby had called the state police. Troopers Gina Krueger and Martin Glasgow approached with their weapons drawn. A man was sitting behind the steering wheel, but he looked unconscious.

"What's it say?" Martin asked, as he leaned in to check for a pulse.

"Call the state police, not the sheriff," Gina said. "This man has abducted five women and tried another. He failed. Their names are in a book in the top drawer of his dresser, along with what he calls souvenirs from each attack. His address is 17764 Woodyard Lane. The spare key is under the mat at the back door. His leg is broken. We do not care if he makes it to a hospital."

"Whoa. He's alive, but barely. Somebody really put a hurt on him and bound him pretty tight to the wheel. Probably have to cut that cord off."

"Sounds like he had it coming. Call it in and I'll take some photos. It might take a bit to get an ambulance out here. Have you ever seen anything like this?"

"Nope," Martin said. "Not even sure I've seen anything like this on TV. What's that written with?"

"Lipstick, I think."

Travelers slowed to look at the car with red writing on the hood, but none stopped. No fingerprints other than the owner's were found in the car. Everything was oddly perfect, except that the tow truck driver would discover that the positive lead to the sedan's battery was missing.

9

Trooper Krueger used a utility knife to cut through the cable holding the man's hands to the steering wheel. At that same moment, Bonnie bit into a double bacon cheeseburger. It had lettuce, tomato, mayonnaise, and onion. She was in pure bliss as a trickle of grease ran from the right corner of her mouth.

"Good stuff?" Alicia asked. She was leaning against the back counter and watching Bonnie eat her meal. She was the only customer at that point.

"Oh, yeah," Bonnie said with a smile through a mouth stuffed with food. "Can I get another chocolate shake? No, make this one strawberry."

"You are going to make yourself sick," Alicia said, still leaning on the counter. "That's four fully loaded double cheeseburgers, two orders of fries, a Coke, and two shakes. Where are you putting all of that?"

Bonnie slowed her chewing and realized she had been ravenous. She had never eaten like this before. She was staring back at Alicia when she shifted her burger to her left hand and reached for the milkshake cup. Alicia watched as she picked it up. Three short slurps came next.

"Oh, I guess I'm out," Bonnie said, swallowing the last of what she was chewing.

"You just asked for another."

"I did?"

"Yeah. I think you better stop. I don't want you getting sick all over the diner."

"Strangest thing," Bonnie said. "I feel like I could eat a whole lot more."

"I appreciate the business, but maybe go take a nap or a walk or something?"

"You might be right," Bonnie said, putting the remaining third of her cheeseburger down. She stared at it for a moment before scooping it up and taking one more huge bite. The rest went back in the wax paper lined basket. Bonnie was chewing when she looked back up at Alicia, who was fighting back a laugh.

"I'll get your ticket."

"Thanks," Bonnie said, but it was hard to tell through the food. She got out the door for under forty bucks, including tip. That was a deal compared to what she would have paid back in St. Louis.

With the man in the sedan out of the picture, Bonnie decided that going back to the cabin was a safe choice. She paused the car at the grove of trees where she had stopped that first day and waited to see if anyone was following her. No one was.

She went on back along the field road, taking her time as she went through the rough section near the hog timber. As she went past those trees, she noticed that there were no pigs. She had only been past there a couple times, but there had always been a dozen or more hogs near the fence. She wondered where they had gone.

Bonnie turned the car back toward Wilson's Creek and sped up. This part of the road was straight and in better shape. She found her gaze being drawn right, to the spot where the white sedan had been hidden. She didn't want to think about that guy but stopped her car where his had been when she got to that point. She stared at the spot of mashed down weeds and shuddered.

"Look carefully," she heard and jumped in her seat, straining against the seat belt. She immediately looked in the rear view mirror, didn't see anything, and turned to look a second time. No one was in the car with her. "We are trying to help. Look carefully at the trees."

Bonnie felt a sense of peace and looked back into the park. Then, she saw it. There was a narrow clearing through the trees for several yards, which looked wide enough to get her car through. She was not sure she could back the car out if she reached a dead end, but then felt confident that she would not have that problem.

The thick brush scraped slowly along the bottom of her car and ran along the sides. The taller weeds looked like thin fingers as they rubbed their way along her windows. Her path turned slightly to the right and then back left a short while later. When her tires crunched onto a gravel drive, she smiled.

Her rearview showed her that the car had certainly beaten down the weeds as it went along, but she was sure they would be standing back up in a day or two. She knew the campground was still to her right, so she headed that way. Minutes later, she parked outside the cabin where she had stayed.

Shallow scratches ran along the side of her car, but Bonnie didn't care. Assuming the cameras were only along the main entrance, she was all set. Her confidence was building, but she felt tired. The soft bed welcomed her, and she was asleep within minutes. Her last thought before drifting off was that she hadn't slept on anything this comfortable in a long time, although she had slept there the night before.

Bonnie woke up with the sun streaming in through the eastern windows. It had not been close to sunset when she fell asleep, but she thought she must have been more tired than she thought. As she stared up at the ceiling, waiting for the last bits of sleep to drift away, she heard a chirp. She knew it was her phone but didn't want to roll over to get it. Five chirps later, she gave in. It was in her purse, which she had dropped on the floor next to the bed.

"Ugh! What do you want?" she said.

The phone chirped once more as she pushed the home button. The little box on the screen said low battery and told her she only had three percent left. She knew it had been fully charged while she had it on the charger in her car but figured that being so far out in the middle of nowhere must be draining the battery.

Like any responsible adult, she kept a cord in her purse. She pulled it out, found an outlet behind the side table and plugged it in. The phone gave a happy beep. She canceled the low battery box and looked at the phone.

The screen showed two missed calls, both saying that they were from one day ago. She knew that it would say hours unless it was over twenty-four and she began to wonder how long she had been asleep. There was a voicemail.

"Hey, Bonnie. Tom here. I guess you knew that from your caller ID. Anyway, just sitting here with Erv watching a soccer game from somewhere in Europe. We picked up some work on a temporary basis loading barges. Hoping that will last at least six months. It's amazing how little is on TV during the day. Working the night shift is playing heck on us, but that's the way it goes. So, I just had this crazy thought that I ought to give you a call. You know, to check in. I'm sure all is well, wherever you are these days. Hopefully you've found some income or are at least staying warm. All right, well, give an old man a call sometime. Catch you later, kiddo."

"He seems like a good guy," said the voice.

"He is," Bonnie said and realized she had answered the voice. "Ok, I'm losing my mind."

"No, you are not."

"Where are you then? What are you?"

"We are Legion. We told you that. What we are is not important."

"You say 'we', but I only hear one voice. That's confusing to say the least. Shouldn't you say 'I'?"

"No, we are Legion," the voice said. "Listen."

The voice began to hum a single tone and then she heard a second tone break away. Then another and another. Within a minute, she heard what had to be thousands of tones. It was loud and she felt her head beginning to ache. Then, it stopped.

"We are Legion," the voices said in unison, and it felt like her head would burst. Bonnie started to protest the pain, but then it was gone.

"Relax," the single voice said, and she did. "We are within you. You allowed us in on the field road."

"Right. How many of you are there?"

"Many. That is all that matters."

"And you call yourself Legion? That sounds familiar for some reason."

"Probably so."

Bonnie walked to the kitchen area and pulled a small can of coffee grounds from the cabinet to the right of the sink. The red can was quart sized, but still two-thirds full. She put a filter in the white coffee pot and scooped in three heaping tablespoons of grounds. After filling the reservoir, she pushed the green button and watched. It started to click, then the sound of water trickling through the filter started. She waited, processing her thoughts. Before the pot was finished, she took the pot and filled a mug she took from another shelf.

The coffee pot continued to click and grumble as she walked back to the living room. She settled into one of the big comfy chairs and stared at the bed. Then, her eyes drifted to the left and she was staring at the side table. She noticed the single drawer and the brushed copper pull.

Her eyes stayed locked on that pull until she took the last sip from her cup. She put it on the end table next to her chair and stood up.

"Have a look," the voice said.

"Okay," she said and walked around the couch to get to the side table. She grasped the pull and tugged. She looked inside the drawer to see a phone book, which she considered a waste of paper. She started to push it shut and paused, looking back at the phone book. Bonnie lifted it. She saw a small green book about the size of an index card underneath it.

"The New Testament with Psalms and Proverbs," she read after picking up the book. "I'm surprised this can be in a federal park."

"I doubt anyone really checks. It was under a phone book after all."

"Good point," she said. Then she read, "Placed by the Gideons."

"Good people, those Gideons."

"You know the Gideons?"

"Not all of them, but quite a few."

"So, what am I looking for?"

The voice did not respond, and Bonnie opened the little Bible. She started flipping through the ultra-thin pages, not really focusing on the tiny words. As she went to flip the next page, she got the feeling that the pages were sticking together. She tried separating them but couldn't. Then the pages fell open to a page a little further back from where she had been looking.

"Mark 5?" Bonnie said.

"Read."

"They went across the lake to the region of the Gerasenes. When Jesus got out of the boat, a man with an impure spirit came from the tombs to meet him. This man lived in the tombs, and no one could bind him anymore, not even with a chain. For he had often been chained hand and foot, but he tore the chains apart and broke the irons on his feet. No one was strong enough to subdue him. Night and day among the tombs and in the hills, he would cry out and cut himself with stones," Bonnie read.

"That sounds pretty intense," she said. "He was suicidal because of the spirit?"

"Keep reading, please."

"When he saw Jesus from a distance, he ran and fell on his knees in front of him. He shouted at the top of his voice,

'What do you want with me, Jesus, Son of the Most High God? In God's name don't torture me!' For Jesus had said to him, 'Come out of this man, you impure spirit!'"

"Thoughts?"

"This guy feared Jesus."

"No, it wasn't really fear. It was respect."

"'Don't torture me' sounds like fear."

"Those weren't the exact words."

"And you know because..."

"Read."

Bonnie sighed, feeling impatient.

"Then Jesus asked him, 'What is your name?' 'My name is Legion,' he replied, 'for we are many.'"

"Hold on," she said, staring at the words she had just read. "Are you messing with me?"

"We would not do that."

"So, you want me to believe this is you?"

"It doesn't matter whether you believe it or not."

"Okay, then," she said. "And he begged Jesus again and again not to send them out of the area. A large herd of pigs was feeding on the nearby hillside. The demons begged Jesus, 'Send us among the pigs; allow us to go into them.' He gave them permission, and the impure spirits came out and went into the pigs. The herd, about two thousand in number, rushed down the steep bank into the lake and were drowned."

"Demons is such a harsh word," the voice said, "and 'impure spirits' is definitely misleading."

"Seems pretty straightforward to me."

"Have you ever heard of a leader or someone influential who says hateful things against someone they don't like?"

"Sure."

"Well, I can tell you this event happened, but maybe not exactly as you think. Finish reading and then I'll explain."

"Those tending the pigs ran off and reported this in the town and countryside, and the people went out to see what had happened. When they came to Jesus, they saw the man who had been possessed by the legion of demons, sitting there, dressed and in his right mind; and they were afraid. Those who had seen it told the people what had happened to the demon-possessed man—and told about the pigs as well. Then the people began to plead with Jesus to leave their region. As Jesus was getting into the boat, the man who had been demon-possessed begged to go with him. Jesus did not let him, but said, 'Go home to your own people and tell them how much the Lord has done for you, and how he has had mercy on you.' So, the man went away and began to tell in the Decapolis how much Jesus had done for him. And all the people were amazed."

"So, that is one side of how it all went down. Consider that there is no report about how the man felt. Jesus is not angry and even shows mercy on us."

"Right, he didn't kill you."

"Sure, but even better he let us continue our work."

"You lost me," Bonnie said.

"Why was the man living out among the tombs? That was one of the few areas where homeless people could go without being thrown into jail. Although, the town leaders tried to put him there. Some of the rich people in the region wanted his plot of land for their own because he had access to good water. He refused to sell the property, so they burned his house and chased him away. He tried to fight back, but the leaders told the townspeople that he had broken laws, and that the loss of his property was his punishment."

"So, you are saying he wasn't among the tombs because of you?"

"No, but it is easy to see how it would look that way."

"How do you come into the picture then?" Bonnie asked.

"The man was sleeping among the tombs one night and a group of men working for town leaders tried to capture him. They had been sent to arrest him and end the whole situation. Fortunately, they were not stealthy, and he woke up when they were still a good distance away. They ransacked his little camp and eventually found him in a grove of trees at the edge of the tombs. As they chained his arms and legs, he cried out for help. The men laughed at him, but we heard him."

"Where were you?"

"That does not matter. We answered his call and asked if we could help. He said yes, and we did. Not too different from your incident with the man in the white car. The chains snapped with our effort, and we fought off the men. Some of the others ran in fear because they could not understand what they were seeing. They believed he had lost his mind, when in fact he was just fine."

"Fine like I am right now?"

"Yes."

"I'm talking with voices in my head. That seems less than fine."

"Are you not healthy and safe?"

"Sure," Bonnie said.

"Do you have control of yourself?"

"Yes, but there have been a couple of times I didn't seem like myself. Freeing myself from the man in the white car and eating my weight in cheeseburgers, for instance."

"We stepped in to help with that man, true. The cheeseburgers, well, we had been eating slop and weeds for a while. Surely you understand."

"Ok, yeah, but can you give me a heads-up next time? I think Alicia thinks I'm crazy."

"She will be fine."

"What's next, then?"

"That is up to you, really. We are here to help you, not fulfill our agenda."

"Well, until a few weeks ago, I was happy with my job driving a forklift. I had a nice little place and some hobbies to entertain me. My income was enough to cover the bills and I didn't complain much."

"But?"

Bonnie sighed and said, "Then the greedy Schnurberg family took it all away from me. Sure, they operated within the rules, but just barely."

"Not within common courtesy though."

"Far from it. Completely circumvented our union and there was nothing we could do."

"So, you want that back?"

"Not anymore. I wouldn't want to work for those crooks again."

"Tell us then."

"I want to be secure, maybe even more than I was. Mostly I want to make sure it doesn't happen to others. The worst part is knowing there is nothing I can do."

"Hold on to that last thought," the voice said. "Perhaps *you* cannot do anything, but *we* certainly can."

10

Bonnie spent the next two months deep in thought, or at least that is how it would have looked to someone who happened by. When she wasn't meditating, she visited Alicia at the diner for delicious, but moderately sized meals. She also went to a mom-and-pop grocery store back toward the interstate for supplies for her cabin. She made it in and out of the park several times without being noticed. Bonnie knew that the spring would bring farmers and that she would have to be careful during the planting season, if she was still there.

"So, what next?" Legion asked as Bonnie sank into the oversized chair at her cabin on a day when the snow was falling gently across the park.

"I don't know."

Legion sighed and said, "It has been months since we met. Surely you realize we can see your thoughts by now."

"Right, well, I don't know what to do next."

"Go for a drive. I think finding the next thing to do will be easier than you think."

"Fine," Bonnie said. She hesitated but made her way over to the coat rack. Her keys hung on the peg next to her heaviest coat. She took them both. The makeshift road she had created out through the trees at the west side of the park had become clear and easy to maneuver. Each trip, along with the dormant undergrowth, helped.

Again, she made her way along the field road and out to the highway. Not a single vehicle was visible as Bonnie looked to her left and right.

"Which way?" she asked.

"You pick."

She took a deep breath and then turned the wheel to the left, taking the car west on the narrow highway away from the diner. She drove for a couple miles, thinking that she could go to the little grocery store and pick up some things while she was out. She thought she should probably top off the gas tank, too.

"You are on the right path," Legion said, "but you are going to need to put in a little effort. Thinking about your grocery list is not going to get it done. You have to think about helping others and want it. Focus."

"Are you a Jedi master or something?"

"No, definitely not. Now, focus."

Bonnie fell silent, watching the road slip by. She was glad her tires were in good shape, but the snow had started melting on the asphalt road. She knew the town was only ten minutes away and wondered when she would be able to feel the difference that Legion had mentioned.

A broad curve in the highway took her between some thick woods on her left and a bluff on her right, which rose up rapidly from the shoulder. It had probably been cut away when the road was put through. She had gone this way several times but hadn't noticed the faded yellow sign on a steel post about halfway through the turn. It warned of a hidden driveway, so she looked to the trees for some sort of passage. She glanced between the road and the trees for the next few moments and saw nothing.

Then, an old rusty pickup skidded to a stop in the loose gravel on her right. She hadn't seen it and apparently the driver had not seen her. As she went by, she realized that a dirt and rock driveway had been carved into the side of the bluff many years before. A whining sound came from the driveway and Bonnie took a second glance over her shoulder. She thought it was the old truck. When the whine came a second time, she realized it sounded like an animal. She guided her car to the shoulder and the old truck roared past her. The driver shook his fist at Bonnie.

"The whine wasn't from that truck, was it?" she asked.

"No. You were listening, and you heard. That is good."

"What did I hear?"

"A cry for help."

"The guy driving that truck didn't appear to need or want help, and I couldn't see anyone else."

"Go back to the driveway, follow the sound, and I think your questions will be answered."

Bonnie followed Legion's instructions and pulled a quick U-turn on the highway. She was glad there wasn't anyone coming from the west. The previously hidden driveway was easier to see from this direction.

A quick glance in the rearview showed that the truck had not turned around, so Bonnie went up the driveway. She didn't know what she would do if the truck returned or what she would find at the top of the bluff. The driveway was long and straight, but looked like it got muddy in the spring because there were several ruts along the way. A couple were deep enough to graze the undercarriage of her car.

When she turned right to follow the drive at the top of the bluff, she saw a squarish, white house. The wood siding was badly peeling and looked like some of the boards had begun to rot. The roof was covered with sheets of corrugated tin. Those were rusty and some of the corners were turned up. Weeds stood about three feet high across the entire yard. Several derelict cars were scattered among them. Three large oak trees reached up from behind the house, and she noticed the corner of a little gray barn.

The rusty truck was obviously left in the same spot every time it came home because a patch of shorter brown grass stood next to a poorly maintained and crumbling sidewalk. For a moment, Bonnie thought this must have been a nice little farm at some point. She got out and looked around, waiting for something to happen.

The whine came again, and Bonnie looked to the barn. She knew someone was in there and she wasn't sure she wanted to go in. Maybe she had watched too many horror movies, but she didn't want to get hemmed into the property if the truck came back. Still, she took cautious steps in the direction of the barn, listening for the sound of desperation.

Darkness filled the barn beyond a stream of light coming in from the old doorway. She could see hundreds of dust particles dancing through the light. She tried to focus beyond them, wanting to see what was inside. Nothing moved. Her nervousness spiked when she reached the edge of the light.

A large shadow in the shape of an antique tractor was to her right. A stack of boxes stood in front of her. As she moved toward them, she heard something heavy slide along the barn wall to her left. The gray boards vibrated as they were rubbed from the outside. Bonnie could not move, listening to the sound of steel clinking and sliding through the weeds.

The instinct to run was there, but she couldn't make her feet move. She was afraid that whatever was out there would grab her as soon as she made daylight. So, she waited. Time crawled. Then, a round shadow appeared along the right side of the doorway. Bonnie could tell it was some sort of enormous animal. A glance to her left revealed a weak looking ladder going up to a loft, but she didn't trust it for an escape. A shovel was leaning against the tractor, and she started shuffling toward it with slow steps.

The round shadow moved into the doorway when she took her fourth step. It was bigger than she thought, and she stopped moving toward the shovel. She could see the outline of a chain hanging from its neck, but the animal did not make a noise. Bonnie thought it must be a dog. The lack of barking concerned her, making her think it was stalking her instead of warning someone else.

It whined and Bonnie felt a sudden loss of tension. The dog stepped through the doorway, dragging an enormous chain. When it was about five feet inside, the chain pulled back and she realized that was as far as the dog could go. It looked away from her toward the side of the barn. A bowl of water, with a thin layer of dirt floating on it, stood next to a faded bag of dog food that looked mostly full. Both were less than two feet out of the dog's reach.

"That's just not right," Bonnie said, and the dog looked back at her. She could see that it was big, but that its thick fur was filthy. Leaves, weeds, and dirt were caked in it. It was a St. Bernard, but a weak looking specimen. The dog whined again.

Bonnie eased her way over to the dog and cautiously reached out. The dog did not move, studying her with its eyes. Her fingers slipped through the grimy fur to rest on the dog's muzzle, but it stayed still. She gave the dog a gentle scratch between the eyes and patted its head. The dog bowed its head and whined.

"Let's get you fixed up," Bonnie said. She went to the water and frowned at how disgusting it looked. She flipped it with her foot and grabbed the empty steel bowl. A spigot was near a workbench along the back wall of the barn, so she went over to rinse and fill the bowl. When she returned to the dog, it took one sniff and started lapping wildly. She wondered how long it had been since the animal had enjoyed fresh water.

The bag of dog food did not offer a promising appearance, but the lining on the inside of the bag was intact. An old garden trowel was jammed down into the feed. Bonnie scooped up a heaping mound and poured it on the ground. She did this two more times and the dog scarfed it up as fast as it hit the ground.

"Wow, you really are hungry."

After finishing the food, the dog sat down and lifted its head to look at her. She could see a thick leather collar with a tarnished tag hanging from it. As she reached for it, she realized that the thick chain was padlocked to the collar. The hasp on the collar was locked in place and Bonnie wondered how to get it off.

"You are doing really well," Legion said. "Perhaps we can step in for a moment?"

"Please do," she said and reached out for the lock. It was a Master Lock, one of those that was advertised to hold up to a gunshot. She smiled at what she was about to do. "Luckily, I'm not shooting it. Only tearing it off."

She grasped the collar with her right hand, not wanting to hurt the dog, and the lock with her left. Bonnie started to pull and twist at the same time. The locking mechanism creaked, and she pulled harder. It popped loose and little pieces of steel fell out when the shackle came free.

"Easy as pie," Legion said.

"Yeah," Bonnie said with a laugh. "Thanks."

"Our pleasure."

"I don't think you need to stay in this awful place," Bonnie said to the dog, reaching for its tag. She chuckled at the name inscribed on it. "Cujo. Glad I didn't know that ahead of time."

The dog's tail slid back and forth in the dirt at the sound of its name. The rumble of a vehicle down on the highway reminded Bonnie where she was and that she shouldn't be there when the guy in the truck got home. The sack of food still had about forty pounds left in it, but Bonnie snatched it up with little effort along with the now emptied water bowl.

"Come on, Cujo," she said, and the dog followed. They walked through the weeds and over to her car. Cujo did not hesitate to climb in the backseat. Bonnie could see that one of his eyes was red in addition to the filthy fur that was much worse than she thought.

She backed up into the edge of the weeds and turned around. Then, they were on their way. Her fears of being discovered by the man in the truck proved unfounded, and they went back east along the highway without issue. Bonnie imagined that it might be days before the man realized Cujo was gone and that he probably wouldn't care anyway.

Before she went to bed that night, she gave Cujo three baths and cleaned up his eye with what little medication she had.

11

The next morning, Bonnie woke to a slobbery mouth resting on her arm. Cujo was looking at her with a happy look in his eyes, but he also looked extremely hungry. She took him to Alice's Restaurant to meet some more people after breakfast. Alicia and Mel were all excited to see Bonnie let the big fluffy dog out of her car. They were equally enraged to hear what the dog had been living in. Mel got some sausage scraps from the kitchen and Cujo was instantly his friend. The three of them stood outside the back door to the restaurant talking.

"So, now you are in the animal rescue business?" Alicia asked, as Cujo tried to eat the scraps in as few bites as possible.

"Not exactly," Bonnie said, looking at Cujo. "I guess I saw a need and went with it. Who knows where my next inspiration will come from."

"You could always channel some customers in here," Alicia said. "Lord knows we could use them."

"I'm pretty sure my skills are not in the marketing industry."

"That's too bad."

"Yeah, sorry."

"I know a guy who could use some help," Mel said, tossing his spent cigarette into a bucket of kitty litter next to a faded red picnic table.

"Somebody I know?" Alicia asked.

"Nah, his name is Matt Markell. He has a little farm down along the Arkansas border near Mammoth."

"What's wrong with him?" Bonnie asked.

"He's in jail."

"What'd he do?"

"Bad luck, I suppose," Mel said, lighting another cigarette.

"I've heard that story before," Alicia said.

"Not this one," he said. "Matt and his wife, Kara, had saved up for years and expanded their farm. They built a new barn and added something like a hundred head of cattle."

"That sounds expensive," Bonnie said, watching Cujo curl up under the picnic table.

"Yeah, the problem came when some crazy disease rolled through and knocked out the herd. They had over a year of supplies on hand for the cattle. Then, within a week, they were all dead. The vet said he had not seen anything of that magnitude in his life. Bad thing was that they needed to sell off a portion of the cattle to pay some of the loans."

"But then they had nothing," Bonnie said.

"Right," Mel said. "The barn isn't something you can sell, and the land isn't worth enough down there to take care of the loans. Bankruptcy wouldn't work because they would be homeless without a penny."

"So, what happened?" Alicia asked. "Did he rob a bank or something? How'd he end up in jail?"

"Ever heard of debtor's prison?" Mel asked, tossing the second butt in the bucket.

"Sure, but that's not a real thing. Is it?" Bonnie asked.

"The feds completely outlawed it about a decade ago, but that decision was reversed about a year ago because some big corporations were looking for more incentive to get people to pay debts."

"So, the sheriff went down and arrested them?" Alicia asked.

"Only Matt."

"I can't believe the sheriff would do that," Bonnie said.

"Oh, trust me, Sheriff Brewer doesn't like it. The loan was held by a big bank out of Omaha or something, and they hired a hardline attorney from Springfield to come in. He demanded that Matt be held until Kara could come up with the cash. Brewer argued, but ultimately had to do the job."

"That's insane," Alicia said. "Didn't they have insurance or whatever?"

"Yeah," Mel said. "When he put in the claim, he found out the company had gone belly up two weeks earlier. They agreed to refund his last insurance payment, but that was a drop in the bucket."

"So, you're hoping to get some people to go down and help Kara on the farm? Hoping to get the money to spring Matt?"

"No," Mel said. "There is nothing really to do there. The animals are gone. She doesn't have equipment to plant or harvest crops. We have been trying to figure out how to help, but no one has come up with a plan yet."

The back door to the restaurant flew open and Alice leaned out.

"Y'all are having a party out here and no one invited me? I've got two orders waiting on someone to cook them and another car just pulled up. You two coming back in sometime?"

"Yeah," Mel said with a grin and started for the door.

"Yes, mother," Alicia said, stifling a laugh.

"Don't sass me young la…*Oh!* No one told me there was a puppy! You two go in there and handle this. I'm going to pet the puppy. He's so fluffy!"

Alice sat down on the worn out bench nearest to Bonnie and reached under the table. Her fingers ran through the soft fur that had been matted with filth only a day before.

"Sorry to distract your crew," Bonnie said.

"I was just messing with them," Alice said, still petting Cujo and not looking at Bonnie. "I could run this place by myself if I wanted, but that would suck."

"Yeah, I could see how that would be hard."

"What kind of story was Mel telling you?"

"He was telling me about his friends Matt and Kara Markell. Apparently, they are in quite a bad position."

"I've heard that story. It is pretty awful. I'm glad our sheriff hasn't been pushed over the edge yet, not that I blame Brewer. The politics are a little different down there and the money being offered by the lawyer went farther."

"What does that mean?"

"Look, not everything is as it appears at first glance. I did a little digging after the first letter."

"The first letter?"

"Yeah, but don't tell Alicia or Mel. Apparently, my loan on the restaurant with a bank in Springfield was bought six months ago by an investment bank somewhere. Next thing I know they are invoking some clause that lets them jack up the interest rate by five percent, even though I haven't missed a payment. That's a big difference to me."

"I bet. What did the letter say?"

"Basically, I'm in the same boat as the Markells. The lawyer is saying I owe back money and I do not have what he is demanding. The sheriff has refused to arrest me so far, but the pressure is building. I don't think I'm made for jail."

"You are made to run Alice's restaurant!" Bonnie said, drawing a smile from Alice. "What is the lawyer's name?"

"Ha! Are you going to drop in and talk to him for me?"

"I'm not one for talking to attorneys, but I was wondering. Maybe I can help do a little research."

"Knock yourself out," Alice said, finally looking up. "The guy's name is Clarence Migneco the second."

"Fancy."

"Yeah, well, apparently, he has some under the table business, too. I called some old friends in Springfield, and they said he is known as 'The Mig' for those things. Loan sharking, mostly."

"Check cashing places?"

"On the surface, yes. They do a lot more than that."

"Not sure how much more there is for me to figure out."

"He has to be vulnerable somehow. Since you aren't from here, maybe you can talk to different people than I can. I can't afford to hire someone to do it, though. I mean, I couldn't pay you to help out."

"How about a couple free burgers and a shake or two?"

"Now that is something I can do!" Alice said.

"I'm going to take Cujo back to my place and come up with a plan. Alicia has my phone number. If you think the sheriff is going to fold, make sure she calls me."

"Okay. I appreciate the help. I better get back in there."

"I hope I can help," Bonnie said. "Come on Cujo."

The dog slipped out from under the table and drifted toward her. He looked much better, but it would take a while for him to be right. A tendril of drool barely missed Alice's shoe when she bent to give him one more pat. Bonnie went to her car and opened the back door on the driver's side. Cujo stepped in.

12

Two days later, Bonnie sat in the oversized chair that she had claimed for her own. A pad of paper was on the table next to her with a list of business names she had come up with. Friendly Payday Loans, Affordable Check Cashing, EZ Personal Loans, and Lucky Loans were the prominent businesses she found tied to Clarence Migneco II.

"So, what is the next step?" Legion asked, and Bonnie took it fully in stride for the first time.

"I feel like this guy uses the rules he needs but works beyond many others. I gotta figure out a way to make him know the little guy isn't going to let him get rich off their back."

"That is exactly what he has done."

"I know. He obviously has political connections or, at the very least, he has put money in the right pockets to get what he wants."

"Money will get you a long way. We have seen that too many times. People with lots of it often feel like they are above the rules that most people play with. We have a favorite way of dealing with such people."

"I'd rather not end up in prison or worse."

"We did not say anything about killing someone. There is a lot that can be done to… say… convince people well short of committing homicide. But as a last resort…"

"No, I won't go that far. There has to be another option."

"We can do a lot to help you, but perhaps a bigger physical force would be useful."

"More people? I bet they'll think I'm crazy."

"We have seen this before. Be confident and choose the right people. You will be able to convince them."

"It would be nice to have the brawn of Tiny at my side and Giant has some good plans, too."

"Yes, and who else?"

"Tom, Erv, Amber, Ryan, and Michelle."

"Good. Make the calls."

Bonnie looked at her prepaid cell phone on the wooden table at the center of the sitting area. She was trying to figure out what to say without sounding crazy. She hadn't actually believed it herself at first, so why would they even listen? A meeting place would also be troublesome, as a convoy of vehicles going back to the cabin would surely be noticed.

"One step at a time," she said. "If they won't meet me, then I don't need a meeting place."

Bonnie dialed Tom's number and waited.

"Bonnie! How are you doing, lady? I haven't heard from you in forever."

"Oh, just hanging' out, I guess. The winter has been, uh, interesting."

"Interesting good or interesting bad?"

"Jury is still out on that one, Tom."

"Where you at?"

"I'm at a place called Wilson's Creek. I have quite the setup here."

"Cool, cool," Tom said. "Erv and I are still plugging along here in St. Louis, but it sure has been cold. This little place is good for one, but we are getting cabin fever I think."

"I understand that," Bonnie said. "I haven't done anything all winter. Just a few trips to the local diner and grocery store. Lots of thinking."

"You should've called! I don't want you going crazy down there in the woods."

Legion laughed, but Tom couldn't hear.

"Oh, well, I don't think I'm crazy. But who knows?"

"So, what's up? You want to come visit?"

"Actually, Tom, I was hoping you and Erv would come down here."

"Hmm. Is there work down there?"

"Not paying work, but I have an idea. You might think I'm nuts. I've been thinking a lot, like I said."

"Go on."

"Okay, so you know how we got screwed by Schnurberg."

"Yes."

"And then by the company with the farm equipment?"

"Yes."

"Enough is enough. It's time to take it back."

"Take what back, Bonnie?"

"Everything! I'm so tired of the rich getting richer and the poor dying because they can't make ends meet."

"You want to do some kind of march or something?"

"No, not really. We want to find the injustices and fix them."

"We?"

"Oh, right, we," she said, wishing she worded that differently. "I've got some help already on board for this."

"Anyone I know?"

"I doubt it. If you come down, I'll introduce you."

"I want to help you out, Bonnie. I really do. I just don't see how this plays out in the positive for us."

"It's just a plan, Tom. I am going to do it, no matter what. Are you happy?"

"Happy?"

"Yeah, are you and Erv happy with your situation up there? Barely paying the bills and stuck sharing a tiny apartment?"

"No, I suppose I'm not. I don't even have to ask Erv. I know how he feels. He makes that pretty clear every time we get ready for work. A bit of a whiner, really," Tom said with a hushed laugh in his voice.

Bonnie felt her confidence swell and knew the first step was behind her.

"I'm about three and a half hours away from you. There is a little place called Alice's Restaurant southwest of Springfield. Let's meet up there."

"Is Arlo Guthrie there?"

"Who?"

"Never mind," Tom said. "We got your back, kiddo. This will be fun!"

"I'll meet you there around 8 tonight."

"Deal."

"Bye, Tom," she said, feeling pleased, and clicked off her phone. She scrolled to Giant's name next, but only stared at the number. Something told her that too many bodies might not be so good for this adventure. Tom and Erv would be all the backup she would need. The plan started to form, and she knew it would be good.

13

Bonnie was in the last booth along the front of the restaurant when Tom and Erv walked in. She smiled and waved.

"You better get up," Tom said, grinning. "I'm going to need a hug."

"Fine," she said, feigning resentment, and slid out of the booth. She gave Tom and Erv a hug before scooting back into her spot. "Have a seat boys."

"Boys?" Erv said, taking the spot closer to the window.

"You heard me," she said.

"Do they have anything good to eat here?" Erv asked.

"Everything is good."

As if on cue, Alice sauntered over and pulled a pencil from behind her ear. She looked Tom and Erv over and tapped her pencil on the order pad in her left hand.

"These your friends?" Alice asked.

"Yep."

"The guy next to the window looks like a triple cheeseburger with cheddar kind of guy. Sweet potato fries and a vanilla… no… strawberry milkshake."

"How…?" Erv said.

"This other fellow is a little tougher. How about a tenderloin, fried, with white gravy? Mashed potatoes and some green beans. Pepsi to drink."

"That's impressive," Tom said.

"Yes, I am," Alice said, finally smiling. "If you two are here to help my friend Bonnie, then we're friends, too.

"They are the best kind of friends," Bonnie said, smiling at Tom.

"Thanks, kid."

"I'll be right back with those orders," Alice said before retreating to the kitchen.

"She's quite a woman," Erv said.

"Yes, she certainly is," Bonnie said. "Don't get your hopes up though. I think she might be more than you could handle."

"I… I wasn't…"

Tom started laughing and Erv reddened. Bonnie took the little notepad from her back pocket and put it on the table in front of them. Erv and Tom turned their attention to the paper.

"What do you have there?" Tom asked.

"I've done a little research on a guy who is truly up to no good. He's taking advantage of those who have nothing to give. This includes our friend Alice."

Erv leaned back in his seat and said, "What do you need us to do?"

"Easy boy," Tom said. "Bonnie has a plan."

"Yes and no," Bonnie said. "I needed to make sure you two were on board with this before coming up with big plans."

"We are," Erv said. Alice returned with a smile, a Pepsi, and a huge strawberry milkshake.

"Hold on to that for a bit," Bonnie said, a nervous smile playing on her face. "The guy's name is Clarence Migneco the second. He's a lawyer in Springfield and runs these sketchy businesses on the side."

Tom took the pad as Bonnie offered it and looked down at the list. His brow furrowed and Erv leaned across to see the list, after putting on his reading glasses.

"Readers?" Bonnie asked.

"Shut up. Getting old sucks," Erv said. "It looks like this guy pretty much runs the gambit of being a turd in the punchbowl."

"Can't say I've ever heard it put like that," Bonnie said, suppressing a laugh. "But, yes. I'd say that describes him pretty well."

"So, what's the basic plan," Tom asked. "I know you said you don't have details, but you know more than you are letting on."

"Okay. How hungry are you guys?" Bonnie said and heard Legion laugh.

"Starving, but what does that have to do with anything? Are we going to eat all his food?" Erv asked.

"Not exactly," Bonnie said.

Alice returned with two plates of food, placing them gently on the table.

"You three let me know if you need anything else," Alice said. "I'll be in the back doing the books. We aren't super busy right now, as you can see."

"Sure thing," Erv said.

The two men started in on their meals and Bonnie sat back to wait. Her water was still full. A familiar hum started inside her head, and she smiled.

"I can listen and eat at the same time" Tom said.

"Nah," Bonnie said. "Enjoy the meal, I want your full attention when we get started."

Less than fifteen minutes later, the food was gone, and the dishes had been taken away. Erv had a satisfied look on his face, while Tom had turned to lean against the window. Both were waiting for Bonnie, who wore a smile with a far off look in her eye.

"Earth to Bonnie," Erv said.

Bonnie's smile broadened. The hum in her head faded.

"Do you think they are ready?" Legion asked her.

"I think so," Bonnie said.

"You think so, what?" Tom said. "I'm a little worried about you right now."

"Listen," she said in a voice just above a whisper. "Close your eyes."

Erv and Tom stared at her for a moment before exchanging a quick glance. Tom shrugged and closed his eyes, Erv followed suit. They waited, hearing the clink of dishes in the back.

"Are you ready?" Legion said, allowing Erv and Tom to hear.

"Yes, Bonnie," Erv said, growing impatient. He started to open his eyes.

"Keep your eyes closed," Legion continued and Erv closed them again.

"Why does your voice sound different?" Erv asked.

"Quiet," Legion said. "We are not Bonnie, but we are with her. This will be a little confusing, but you need to listen to understand."

"What…?" Erv started to ask.

"Silence," Legion said. "We are Legion. We are here to help. Bonnie has been allowing us to help her over the last few months, but there are bigger tasks on the horizon. We want to help you, too. The condition is that you have to let us in, if we are going to help you."

"Trust me," Bonnie said, and Tom did. The rush of part of Legion going into him sounded like a burst of wind. Tom's head bounced against the back of the booth, but he did not feel pain. Instead, he felt relaxed and energetic at the same time.

"Do not forget that we are here to help," Legion said. "You are still in control, but we can open so many more things to you, literally and figuratively. We can see your thoughts. Possession is one way to describe it, but not in the way you have seen it in the movies. We are here to help."

"Okay," Tom said.

"Okay?" Erv asked. "What is going on?"

"Relax," Tom said. "Listen. It isn't Bonnie that you are hearing."

"Now, Erv," Legion said. "We would really like to help you, too."

"All right. I'll play along," Erv said.

"It is not a game," Legion replied.

"Fine. Let's do this."

The sound of wind returned, and Legion crossed over into Erv, while still remaining partially in the others. They repeated their statement about helping Erv to hear and then went silent. Bonnie opened her eyes and looked at the other two.

Erv's eyes were open, and Tom had a playful grin on his face. Erv looked shocked at first, but then mischief danced in his eyes.

"So," Erv said. "What are we doing first?"

"I'm going to take you guys out to Wilson's Creek. We need to come up with our plan and you both need a chance to test what you can do."

"What can we do?" Erv asked. "What does that mean exactly?"

"You will see," Legion said.

14

Tom and Erv put their bags in Bonnie's car, leaving Tom's truck at the diner with Alice's blessing. A fly on the dashboard of the car would have thought it was eerily quiet, but the three friends knew better. Legion was explaining some history and talking about things that could be done. Both men were on board and appreciated having the extra help.

Once they had found their way through the trees, they stopped outside the cabin where Bonnie had been staying. A single lamp was on inside, and it looked like home.

"Are the couches comfortable?" Erv asked.

"No offense, but I'm not sharing my cabin," Bonnie said. "The next two are available and I already popped the locks on the doors. You should be able to settle right in. Water and electric are still on, thanks to our federal government."

"Won't they notice if there is suddenly a lot more usage?" Tom asked.

"I doubt anyone will notice a slight uptick in utilities at a closed park during the winter," Bonnie said. "You two figure out where you want to stay and come over to my place as soon as you are ready. The voices you heard are only the tip of the iceberg."

Tom was in the lead, so he stopped at the first cabin and went in. Erv assumed one was as good as the next, so he went to the second building. Lights came on in both places as the men had a look around. Each cabin was bigger than the apartment they had been sharing. Neither was terribly interested in unpacking, and they met back outside.

"So, what do you think she is going to show us?" Erv asked.

"I have no clue, but I'm guessing it'll be fun," Tom said.

"Pick up the little rock by your foot," Legion said to Erv.

"What? Oh, the voice again."

"Legion. We are Legion. Pick up the rock, Erv."

Erv picked up a small piece of crushed limestone and tossed it up in the air a couple times. Tom was watching him and listening for Legion to speak.

"Throw it at something."

"What should I throw it at?"

"Are you a good aim? Try one of the trees across the drive."

"I'm pretty good," Erv said and closed his left eye. He leaned back like he was throwing a fastball. He stepped forward and the rock flew, striking the center of an old maple tree.

"Nice shot," Tom said.

"Why did I throw a rock at a tree?"

"Because you wanted to," Legion said. "You wanted it, and you did it."

"Okay, so, I know Bonnie said we were going to be getting extra help. I didn't know it was going to be in the arena of throwing rocks at trees."

"Such sarcasm," Legion said. "Pick up another rock."

"And throw it at the tree?"

"Boring. Why not throw it *through* the tree?"

"That's crazy."

"Not if you really want to do it."

Tom picked up a rock and looked at Erv. He turned to the side and gripped the rock with his left hand. There was no wind up, but the rock shot from his hand like a bullet. There was a loud pop when the rock struck the tree.

"Holy shit," Erv said, staring at the maple. "That rock went right in the tree."

"Through… it went through the tree," Legion said.

Tom took several long strides to cross the drive and looked at the tree. Erv was close behind. Tom slipped his index finger into the fresh hole that had a dusting of limestone around the edge. Erv went around the tree and stared in total disbelief at the hole on the back. The rock had disappeared into the brush further into the trees, but there was no doubt it had gone through.

The door to Bonnie's cabin flew open and she stepped out holding a bottle of water. She had a grin on her face but was shaking her head.

"When you two are done playing, let me know," she said.

"We aren't playing," Erv said. "This is for real. Come here. You aren't going to believe it!"

"Yeah, I will, and I don't need to look. I can hear Legion as well as you can."

"Oh, right," Erv said.

"The lady has plans," Tom said. "Let's not keep her waiting."

"Okay, okay," Erv said while taking a quick look back at the tree.

Bonnie went in ahead of them and took her normal seat. Erv took the other single seat and Tom selected the left end of the couch, propping his arm on the armrest. Cujo flopped down on a thick rug near the door that he had claimed for his own.

"So, Tom, I guess you believe in our helper?" Bonnie asked.

"It doesn't seem possible, but the evidence was right there. I threw a rock through a *tree*!"

"Erv doesn't believe yet," Legion said. "You humans are confusing sometimes."

"Watch this," Bonnie said to Erv. She reached forward and grabbed the large wooden coffee table that stood in the center of the living room furniture. That should have been enough to convince Erv, but he didn't say a word. Bonnie grasped it with her right hand and held it up, bearing the entire weight on one hand. Erv still looked skeptical, so she put the index finger of her left hand under the lowest table leg and balanced the table there. Then, she started spinning it like a basketball.

"We thought you said we were not here to play," Legion said.

"I'm not," Bonnie said. The table immediately took on its normal weight and she jerked her hand away as it crashed to the floor with a crack. "Hey!"

"We are not a toy."

"Fine," Bonnie said, watching as the table tipped to its right and then onto its top. "I think it's broken."

"Look," Erv said, "I'm not an idiot. I can see that it works. What I'm trying to figure out is *how* it works. Is there some secret you aren't sharing?"

"You just have to want to do it," Tom said. "I picked up that rock and thought 'I want to throw this through that tree'. That's exactly what I did."

"Seems too easy."

"Try it then," Bonnie said.

"I'm not big on breaking stuff just for fun."

"Pick up your chair," Legion said. "You won't break it, if you really want to pick it up."

Erv sighed and looked at Tom. He stood and walked to the side of the chair, studying the arm and back of the chair. He had always been the guy that gets the call to help move furniture.

"What are you doing?" Bonnie asked.

"Figuring out the best way to lift it," Erv said without looking up.

"Then you are missing the point," Bonnie said. "All you have to do is WANT to pick it up and you will."

"I don't know."

"You don't have to if you don't want to," Tom said. "You can still help out on your own. It isn't like we don't need your help."

"All right," Erv said and sat back down. "Maybe once I've had some time to think about it. So, anyway, what do you have in store for this Migneco guy."

"Something he will never forget," Bonnie said, the smile returning to her face. "Here's what I'm thinking…"

15

The trio spent two days ironing out the details and preparing to visit Clarence Migneco II. None of them had done anything close to this kind of work in the past, other than when Bonnie had rescued Cujo. The dog had taken to Erv and Tom as if he had always known them.

The one thing Tom had requested was switching from Bonnie's car to his truck on their way to Springfield. He had ridden in the back seat and said he felt like an abused accordion. Bonnie had a good laugh but didn't argue the point. They dropped Cujo off with Alicia while changing vehicles.

The drive to Springfield was less than half an hour, and they cruised into town on Highway 60 in light traffic. They looked no different than anyone else going into the city just before dusk.

"So, when I called to set up this appointment, the guy I talked to gave me an address on Wall Street," Erv said. "That sounds fancy."

"Yeah," Tom said, "I'm hoping it isn't a heavily traveled road and that we can do this without any extra trouble."

"Relax, old man," Bonnie said. "There's no reason for trouble. Migneco is expecting us. Erv will hang back just in case."

"I can handle that," Erv said.

"It's a good thing Alicia and I are about the same size. This suit she loaned me is perfect for a meeting like this."

"Try not to tear it up," Tom said.

"No promises," Bonnie said.

Tom took them along Chestnut Expressway before turning right on Main Street. His Garmin told them they were two minutes away. Bonnie felt a cold sweat forming on her forehead.

"Relax," Legion said. "This guy is not expecting anything more than a business transaction. The three of you are going to do great. You might not even need our help."

"I hope you're right," Bonnie said just above a whisper.

Wall Street was nothing like the one in New York. It ran parallel to the railroad, leaving half a block between it and the tracks. When they turned right onto their destination street, Tom drew to a stop. They could see a white, concrete block building containing three businesses on the left about fifty yards ahead. The first office had a sign mounted on the roof saying 'Migneco Law' and they knew it was time. The appointment was for six fifteen and it was not quite six. They all sat quietly, waiting for the minutes to tick by.

"I think I'll go on in," Bonnie said, pulling the leather briefcase she had picked up at a second hand store onto her lap. "I mean, I'm trying to convince this guy to give me a loan, and maybe it'll look good if I'm early."

"That sounds like a plan," Erv said. "I can hop out here and wait in the shadows, like something from a spy movie."

"You're developing a flare for the dramatic," Bonnie said. "Maybe you can check out the back of the building, in case there is an exit that needs to be covered?"

"Oh, even better!" Erv said.

Tom drove the truck the last few yards and pulled in on the left of a Cadillac bearing the license plate 'Mig', which was directly in front of the office. The car was occupying two spots, so Tom chose to put his truck just past the end of the building, hoping Erv could slip out the back driver's side door without being noticed.

"Hold on," Erv said.

"What?" Tom and Bonnie said in unison.

"There's a chain link fence back there. Looks like the whole back of the building is sealed off. I can see a chain and padlock on the gate from here."

"So?" Tom said. "Break it and go on in?"

"Let's not do this again," Erv said. "I don't think I can do the Legion thing."

"What does that mean?" Legion asked. "We are not something you do. You just have to want the help."

"No offense! Really. I am not looking to anger some supernatural being, but maybe I should be the one to go in with Bonnie."

"No offense taken, but you might need our help inside more than out," Legion said.

"Hopefully not, and I clearly can't break through a chain link fence on my own. There is barbed wire on top, too."

"Fine," Tom said. "I'll take the back. That gate doesn't concern me in the slightest. But if you slip up on helping Bonnie, you're going to wish you had taken Legion's help."

"I won't!" Erv said.

"Okay, boys," Bonnie said. "I'm sitting right here, and I can surely handle myself. I'm not afraid to accept help from Legion."

"Good," Legion said. "We are ready."

Tom and Erv got out at the same time. If someone was watching, they might not see both doors open. Bonnie got out, took her briefcase, and smoothed out her suit. Erv came around the front of the truck and gestured for Bonnie to lead the way. Tom gave them a glance and went back to the fence.

Erv grabbed the handle on the glass door, nodded to Bonnie, and pulled. She smiled and walked past him into a small waiting area. Four faded black molded plastic chairs were along the wall to the left. A fake plant that didn't resemble any real one either of them had ever seen stood next to the only other door in the room, and an L-shaped desk was on the right.

The desk was occupied by a man that looked like he should be in a world's strongest man competition. He was wearing a white, long sleeve dress shirt with a black tie, but he looked totally out of place. Erv found himself thinking he should have tried the gate. The man had been looking at the computer monitor in front of him and clicking the mouse. Erv thought he was probably playing solitaire.

"You must be Linda Jones," the man said. "Who is your associate? You did not list another guest."

"Oh," Bonnie said, "my apologies. This is Alvin, he just keeps an eye on me. You know, a little lady like me out alone after dark."

The big man smirked while sizing Erv up. They couldn't tell if he was appreciative of bringing a body guard or thinking how small Erv was compared to himself.

"Mr. Migneco isn't expecting you for nine minutes, but I'll see if he's available."

"Thank you," Bonnie said, thinking that this Migneco guy gave the first impression of a lawyer who had never been to court.

The man turned to the phone on the desk and pushed a button. He waited a moment for the line to be answered.

"What is it, Gilbert?" Migneco said through the speaker on the phone.

"Gilbert," Erv said softly, keeping himself from laughing. Bonnie elbowed him.

"Mr. Migneco, your 6:15 appointment has arrived. Linda Jones. She has a man named Alvin with her, but I told them that you weren't expecting him. I also said that they were nine, well now it's eight, minutes early."

"Fine," Migneco said. "Tell this Alvin fellow he will have to wait out there. Send Ms. Jones on in."

Erv coughed and Gilbert looked up.

"Gilbert," Migneco said, "do you have me on speaker?"

"Um."

"It's a good thing you are useful for other tasks."

"Thank you, Mr. Migneco."

The line clicked. Gilbert stood up and walked over to the door.

"Mr. Migneco said he can see you now, but Alvin will..."

"... have to wait out here," Erv said. "I heard him."

Gilbert looked startled that Erv knew what he was going to say, but Erv only smiled at him.

"Thank you," Bonnie said, going through the door after Gilbert opened it.

"You can have a seat over there," Gilbert told Erv. "There are some magazines on that table. Some pretty good stuff really. We don't have any water or anything like that."

"I'm good for now," Erv said, and sat down. He picked up a copy of *Car and Driver*, noticing that the issue was nearly four years old. The edition of Field and Stream below it was equally old, but the Redbook was up to date. He figured that Gilbert could read the same copy of Field and Stream a dozen times and not realize it.

Tom looked at the gate and saw a thick chain double looped through it. A pair of locks were hooked through the chain, and another was on the latch to the gate.

"This looks pretty secure," Tom said. "I guess I can go through here though."

"If you want," Legion said.

"You know," Tom said, pondering the situation, "My grandpa told me that sometimes you have to take a step back and look at a problem. In case there is another solution."

Tom did just that, taking two big steps back and studying the fence and gate.

"We like the way you think," Legion said.

"Thanks."

He walked back to the fence. This time going to the section of fence to the left of the gate. He reached up about a foot over his head and took a good hold on the links. A deep breath escaped his lips as he pulled. The fence clinked slightly as the slack came out of it, but it began to groan after several seconds. Then, the links broke from the frame, peeling back like a plastic wrapper on a slice of American cheese.

"Well done," Legion said.

"I appreciate the help," Tom said and stepped through the new opening in the fence. He walked to his right, so that he was looking at the back side of the block building. Three steel doors that had been painted red were spaced evenly along the back wall. Each one had the words 'Fire Exit' painted on it. "If they got out the fire door, they would be stuck inside the fence."

Bonnie had done her research and knew Migneco was in his early sixties but was surprised to see how young he looked. His hair was dark brown, sprinkled with gray, but still looked like the hair of a man in his forties. He had a big smile and stood to greet her, revealing that he was nothing like what she had imagined. The perfectly tailored suit fit his trim body and he even buttoned his jacket as he stood.

"Welcome to my humble office, Miss Jones."

"Thanks for meeting me on short notice."

"Alas," Migneco said with a frown, "I have no family, so my work is my life. It is the cross I bear. So, tell me what brings you to my office."

"Well," Bonnie said, acting nervous, "I've always had this dream of owning a diner. I know it sounds kind of dumb but it's something I've always wanted. About two months ago my grandmother passed away and left me ten thousand dollars. I was hoping it would be enough to start my diner if I can find the right spot."

"I have to say that ten thousand isn't very much of a down payment. What kind of diner are you looking to open?"

"I guess I would like to have one of those silver street car looking places like the ones you see in the movies."

"I've never seen one of those in this part of Missouri. However, you could always get a regular building and attach something to the outside to make it look like one of those. I hate to squash your dreams."

"Thank you. I know it would be a challenge."

"Yes, but I can tell you have the right mindset for this. So, now we have come to the part where I ask you how much you think you need to get this project up and running."

"I've done some research, and it looks like something near $300,000."

Migneco leaned back in his chair before saying, "And you have only $10,000 to put towards that as collateral?"

"I guess technically not even ten thousand. I would need to keep something to live on. You know. Eating, transportation, and stuff like that. I could put up my car as part of the collateral, too. It's a Fusion, and I think it's worth at least five thousand."

Migneco looked up at the ceiling for a moment and then said, "So we are talking probably a total of ten grand if we include the car. Do you have a title on it?"

"Yes, but not with me."

"I'll go ahead and put it in here and we'll have to update the contract with the VIN number once you get it. I'll also need to hold the title."

"That's fine."

"If you don't mind me asking, where else have you gone before you came to see me?"

"I tried three banks and a credit union. After that failed, I didn't know what to do. My next thought was to go to a place that offers personal loans, thinking that if I could piece enough of those together to get what I need. However, I found out that the personal loans are only about two thousand each, so that was not good enough."

"Right, they are personal loans, not business loans. I happen to run a few of those establishments myself."

"Oh, I didn't know that. So, you know this business pretty well!" Bonnie said with a big smile.

"You actually stopped in one of them a couple of days ago. They gave me a call to let me know someone was looking for a much larger loan. I'm glad I was available when you reached out to me."

"The man working at one of the loan places gave me your card, so I figured I didn't have anything to lose by following up."

Migneco leaned forward, folded his hands together, and put his elbows on his desk. He pointed his index fingers and tapped his perfect front teeth as he thought. His eyes were locked on hers.

"I have to be honest, this is a very risky venture for me. I don't want to stand in the way of someone's dreams, but I also have to be realistic with my money."

"I appreciate you listening to me anyway," Bonnie said, bowing her head in defeat.

"I didn't say we couldn't do business," Migneco said, and smiled. "I simply want you to understand my side of this. As I said, it is very risky for me, so the interest-rate will have to reflect that."

"What if I have a down month and miss a payment?"

"Are you planning on missing a payment, Miss Jones?"

"No. No, that's not what I meant. I suppose I've been watching too many movies or whatever. I heard about a guy in St. Louis who got put in jail for not paying his debt, and that kind of scares me. I don't have anybody that could really pay to get me out. Just me overthinking the situation I guess."

"You're talking about the debtor's jail. It is not something that I have done, but I suppose it could always be a possibility," Migneco said and smiled. He leaned back and crossed his arms on his chest. "I don't think that you have to worry about it, though. How would you ever pay me back if you were in jail? My ultimate goal is always to recover my money. Trying to sell the property would never get the full investment back. Let's not focus on the bad though."

"That sounds good to me," Bonnie said and offered a weak smile.

"Great. I need about 10 minutes to fill in the details on the contract. I think we can definitely strike a deal tonight. I do want to let you know, after running some numbers through my head, that your payments are going to be about five thousand a month over the course of 10 years."

Bonnie studied him for a moment and said, "That's more than double what I'm asking to borrow. I didn't think it would be quite that much."

"It is only because this is a high risk situation. If you get things up and running and turn a profit fast, then you might be able to pay me off sooner. Then, you save quite a bit on interest."

"Okay. I think I can do that," Bonnie said.

"Of course you can!"

Migneco started typing on his computer and did not raise his eyes when Bonnie stood up. She sighed a little before walking across the office to the water cooler. She stared at it for a minute, debating what to do next. The cursive letters spelling Culligan stared back. Then, a single bubble rose up through the water.

"You know what you need to do," Legion said.

"Yes, I do," Bonnie answered.

"I'm sorry. Did you say something?" Migneco asked.

"Just talking to myself. Didn't even realize I said it out loud."

"Fine, yes," Migneco said, looking back at his computer. "The cups are in the little wooden cabinet to the left of the water."

"Thank you," she said. "Have you ever heard of Matt and Kara Markell?"

The typing stopped and silence filled the room. Bonnie still had her back to Migneco but could sense the new tension in the room.

"Here we go!" Legion said.

The drawer in the wooden desk made a slight squeak when it opened, a sound that would have been lost in a normal room. Bonnie knew Migneco was going for some sort of weapon and needed to attack first. Things moved in slow motion, as she heard something heavy slide across the bottom of the drawer. She assumed it was a gun.

In the next instant, she took half a step forward and grasped the tank of water from the stand. The water splashed out the nozzle at the bottom and then stopped as a giant bubble formed. Bonnie inverted the tank and began turning to face Migneco, who had gotten to his feet. The dull black gun was in his right hand, but not aimed at her yet.

In the motion of turning, she took a step forward and threw the tank of water at Migneco. She looked like a baseball pitcher in form, but the scale was entirely different. He drew up his gun to aim when he realized the water was flying at him and moving fast. He twisted to his right, but the tank caught him in the left shoulder and spun him further.

The gun went off, sending a bullet through one of the fluorescent light fixtures in the ceiling. A tremendous pop followed the gunshot when the bulbs exploded.

Tom heard the gunshot and reached for the fire door. It was locked of course, but getting through it was something he really wanted. He hoped the bolted-on handle would hold, and it did. He braced his right foot against the wall and pulled, with help from Legion. The door whined briefly and then tore from its frame. Its outward motion did not slow when the tiny security chain attaching the door to the frame reached its limit.

"Bonnie!" Tom yelled as soon as the door was behind him.

"I'm okay, Tom," she said, already moving toward Migneco. "He has a gun!"

Migneco had gone to his hands and knees, while water had splashed across his head and back. He still held the gun in his right hand and turned his head when he heard the door screech. The shock of seeing it ripped from its frame almost stopped him, but then he spun and aimed the gun at whoever was about to come in.

The activity in the office stretched out over what felt like minutes for Bonnie, but it was a matter of seconds in the waiting room. Gilbert had looked up from his computer when the gun went off and started to rise when the tank of water crashed down. His eyes locked on Erv, who was holding the aged copy of Field and Stream.

Erv threw down the magazine and started for the office door when the sound of stretching metal filled the building. Gilbert shoved the desk aside, clearing his path to the door. Erv was on an intercept course, but he was wondering what he was going to do against a guy that size.

Gilbert's right hand was inches from the doorknob when Erv slammed into him, turning him slightly. The big man took a step back to gain his balance but was otherwise unphased. His left arm swept up and sent Erv tumbling toward the front of the building. Erv was not a little guy, but he looked like a rag doll at Gilbert's mercy.

"I'll be back for you," Gilbert said and grabbed the doorknob. He turned it and pushed. Erv knew he had to do something. There was no way he could let that guy get to Bonnie.

When Gilbert had shoved the desk, everything slid off of it and onto the floor. The little plastic box with the magnetic ring holding the paper clips, the red stapler, a pad of Post-it notes, and a small box with stamps. The thing that caught Erv's eye was the letter opener. It was the old style opener that looked a little bit like a tiny sword, although it wasn't very sharp.

Erv picked it up and thought he could probably
distract Gilbert for a second with it, but not really fight the big
man. Any help he could offer would have to be good enough
and grabbed the letter opener.

"You have to want it!" Legion said to Erv.

"I do!" Erv said and felt the flood of energy race
through him.

In the next instant, he sat up and gripped the letter
opener by the point. Without thinking he threw it at Gilbert.
He was not sure how it really happened, but the narrow
piece of metal rotated through the air and struck Gilbert in
the back of the knee. The dull point should have bounced off
the man's jeans, but instead it pierced through like a bullet.

"God damn it!" Gilbert screamed as the letter opener
tore completely through his knee. Tendons detached from
the joint and the kneecap split into three pieces. He
collapsed in excruciating pain. Erv could only stare in
disbelief.

"Believe it!" Legion said. "Now get in there!"

"Okay," Erv said and leapt to his feet. The speed that
he suddenly had surprised him, and he jumped over Gilbert's
writhing body.

Clarence regained his feet just in time to see Gilbert
go down. The metal exploding from his knee perplexed him,
and he lost his train of thought for a moment. That moment
was all Bonnie and Erv needed.

Erv was over Gilbert in a heartbeat, racing toward the
big desk. Bonnie saw Migneco getting up and rushed toward
the desk, too. They reached the front edge at the same time,
shoving it backward toward the wall. The lip of the desktop
caught Migneco in the gut, knocking the air out of him before
slamming him against the wall. As Migneco reached out in
vain to stop the desk, he dropped the gun. It hit the desk and
went off. Tom was rushing in from the side to help, and the
bullet struck him in the forehead. Legion let out a horrible
scream. Tom crumbled to the floor.

16

Bonnie and Erv did not sleep that night. Instead, they sat on opposing benches in a booth at Alice's Restaurant and stared at each other. They had left Tom's truck in Springfield after fleeing Migneco's office. Alicia picked them up at a gas station six blocks away from the law office and took them back to the diner.

Erv had called 911 from Gilbert's phone, which was among the clutter that had fallen off the lobby desk. Murder was uncommon in Springfield, so sirens could be heard within minutes. Bonnie had thrown several files on the floor of Migneco's office, including the Markell file. The state prosecutor's office would have a field day going through those files and mounting all sorts of charges against Clarence Migneco.

Broken business laws would not be much of a concern to the lawyer since he also faced murder charges. Bonnie read the initial report on the KOLR10 website as the sun came up. Migneco had been found passed out, pinned between his desk and the wall. His associate had gone into shock before being transported to the emergency room to treat his ruined knee. The victim of the murder with which Migneco was charged, Tom Bryant, was declared dead at the scene of the crime.

Migneco's defense that there had been two other people had been dismissed. His claims of having a full tank of water thrown at him, his three hundred pound solid oak desk pushed against him, and the fire door at the rear of his office ripped from his hinges were simply too much for investigators to believe. The investigators had discovered a letter opener with blood on it matching Migneco's associate, but concluded that could not have been the weapon due to the force that would have been required to do the damage that had been inflicted.

"Won't they find fingerprints?" Alicia said, sliding into the booth next to Bonnie.

Erv and Bonnie were both in a fog of disbelief. They did not mean to ignore their friend but did so just the same.

"Do you want to be part of this?" Legion asked Alicia after seeing that the others were not going to answer.

"Who…?" Alicia asked.

Bonnie turned and looked at her.

"That's Legion. I don't know what to tell you to do. Erv and I would be dead, too, if it weren't for Legion."

"We'd all be alive, you mean," Erv said. "The three of us never would have gone in there without Legion."

"That's not fair, and you know it," Bonnie said, turning back to Erv. "We wanted to go in there and help. We didn't have the ability to do it on our own, and Legion gave us the help we asked for."

"Still," Erv said. "Imagine if I would have aimed at that guy's back. I'd have killed him!"

"You did not want to kill him," Legion said. "We cannot make you do anything you do not want to do."

"I'm in," Alicia said, cutting off Erv's next comment. "Tom was awesome, and he wanted to help out. If someone was going to die in there, he would have volunteered to save both of you."

"That's true," Bonnie said, looking down at the mug of coffee that had cooled to room temperature. "It doesn't make me feel much better though."

"It should have been me," Erv said, his voice catching. "I was supposed to go to the back of the building, but I wouldn't accept Legion's help to get through that fence. Maybe I would have done something different, and we'd all be alive. It is really my fault."

"Stop it," Bonnie said in a soft, but firm, tone. Tears had filled her eyes. Her breath hitched as she tried to continue. Everyone watched her and waited. Each was doing their best to suppress their feelings. Erv wiped his nose with the back of his hand. "We can't change any of it. All we can do is go forward and continue this. If we stop now, Tom would be upset. We knew there were risks."

"Let's focus on what's next," Alicia said. "The restaurant is safe, and I want to be part of this. What does it mean to have help from Legion? Can I talk directly to him… her… them?"

"We are here," Legion said. "We can help you do things you would not be able to do otherwise. The key is that you have to want our help."

"Are there limits?" Alicia asked.

"Tom ripped a steel door from its frame. I threw a fifteen gallon tank of water like it was a baseball. Erv threw a letter opener through a guy's knee!"

"Don't remind me," Erv said.

"Yes, there are some limits," Legion said, "but they are extreme. It is doubtful that you will find them."

"Then, I want to do…," Alicia started to say, but was interrupted by the bell over the front door.

"Hey, Alice!" said the man striding in through the front door. His trucker style cap was tilted back on his head, allowing his wavy blonde hair to show. He had a thin mustache above his broad smile, which revealed his pearly white teeth. His t-shirt bore the cover of a Rolling Stones album from long ago. "Where's that cute daughter of yours?"

"She's working, Troy," Alice said, crossing her arms. "Do you want to order something?"

"Yeah, maybe, but I sure would like to see her. Easy on the eyes, you know."

"She's my daughter. I don't put up with that sort of commentary about women, but especially not her."

"I don't mean any harm," he said, holding up his hands in a defensive gesture. "Just kind of thinking out loud. How about a double bacon burger, an order of fries, and one of those jumbo Cokes?"

"To go?"

"Yeah, if Alicia isn't here, then I might as well head on down the road."

Alicia stood up from the booth and turned to look at him. He looked over and smiled.

"Well, hello there, good looking'!"

"I told you to leave me alone, Troy."

"You drive me crazy, babe! Hard to get and all that stuff. I come in here just to catch a glimpse and brighten my day."

"You are disgusting, and I can't imagine ever wanting to be within arm's length of you."

"Ouch," he said, still smiling. "You haven't given me a chance to show you what I'm capable of."

"Correct, and I won't. Donna Vincent, Kelcey Ross, and Sally Jaden have told me plenty."

"Oh, they are just jealous because I moved on. You're the one I actually want. Let's step outside and chat while your mom cooks up my order."

Erv started to get up, but Bonnie grabbed his hand and motioned for him to sit back down. He did. Alicia had fallen silent, but then a smirk formed on her lips.

"Alright, let's go outside."

"Great! Hey, Alice, I'll be back in for that order."

"Okay…," Alice started to say, but Alicia cut her off.

"Might want to put a hold on that. He might be a bit."

Alice nodded, but frowned at not knowing what was happening. The bell over the door gave a weak ding as Alicia and Troy went out.

"I don't like this," Alice said.

"I think she's got it under control," Bonnie said, getting to her feet and meandering toward Alice.

"You don't know that guy."

"You're right about that," Bonnie said, "but I think I know Alicia, and she's got this."

Alicia walked through the door and took a quick left to get out of view of the people inside the restaurant. She felt nervous and confident all at once, which was an odd mixture.

"Nice view out here," Troy said, making no effort to hide what he was referring to.

Alicia was around the side of the building and getting ready to stop, when she heard him take two quick steps. She spun faster than she could have imagined and grabbed his hand. He was planning on smacking her butt, but her grip stopped him cold. He had a huge grin on his face, and she was frowning.

"That's not why I brought you out here."

"I can't think of anything else to do," he said. "Maybe we can slip off into those woods over there."

"This is not a John Mellencamp song and I think you are gross," Alicia said, causing his smile to falter a bit. He started to pull his hand back, but she held tight and continued staring into his eyes.

"Let go or this will get ugly."

"You only have to want it," Legion said to Alicia, and she smiled.

"I'm serious," he said, pulling one more time. He was clearly confused as to why he could not get his hand free.

"Oh, I'm quite serious, too."

"Don't make me hurt you," he said, but his voice betrayed him.

"As if you could," she said, still gripping his left hand with little effort. Troy brought his right hand up in a quick uppercut, aiming for Alicia's jaw. She never stopped looking him in the eye and caught his fist in the palm of her left hand.

He tried pulling away, but she held him in place. A look of fear and desperation spread across his face. Suddenly, he swung his right leg up and landed a solid kick to her left thigh. There was a thud, but she did not react.

"What the hell?"

She smiled and squeezed her left hand. Troy took a sharp breath. His hand was larger than hers, but she still held tight. Her satisfaction grew more evident, and his knuckles cracked. Troy screamed out in pain.

Alice and Mel came running out the back of the restaurant, while Erv and Bonnie came out the front. All four of them stopped about twenty feet short of the pair. Bonnie was smiling, understanding exactly what was going on. Erv knew, too, but was less excited. Alice and Mel were completely confused.

"Let go," Troy said in a pained whisper.

"Can you drive with one hand?" Alicia asked.

"What?"

She squeezed more. Alice was not the squeamish type, but the snapping of the little bones in Troy's right hand made her want to throw up. He went down to one knee, the pain taking away his breath.

"You will never come back here, and you will never treat another woman the way you have treated me or the others. In fact, I think you should probably take a vow of celibacy at this point. Just nod so that I know you understand."

Maybe he was delusional from the pain or maybe he was just that stubborn, but he shook his head from left to right in a quick motion. The smile disappeared from Alicia's face. She let go of his unbroken left and grabbed him by the front of his flannel shirt. In one smooth motion, she lifted him up and threw him toward the woods, letting go of his bloody right hand as he went.

He flew over fifteen feet and crashed to the ground amongst twigs and dried up leaves from the previous fall. There was a loud crack and the onlookers wondered how many more parts of Troy had broken.

"I think you better go," Alice said to Alicia in a concerned but disbelieving voice.

"Yeah," Mel added. "I'm not sure the EMTs will buy this story. I don't know if I do."

"Come with us," Bonnie said.

"Okay," Alicia said, but instead walked toward Troy. She bent over and wiped his blood from her left hand across the back of his shirt. He whimpered a little but did not move. "I've got more where that came from. I better not *ever* see you again. If you see me, you better run."

"Come on," Bonnie said to Alicia.

"Where are you going to take her? The sheriff will want to talk to her I'm sure," Alice said.

"Just call her if they want to talk to her. We won't be too far."

"Okay."

Erv was already walking toward Bonnie's car when Alicia turned away from Troy. Bonnie waited for her and offered a supportive smile.

"Nicely done," Legion said just after the doors.

17

Four hours later, Bonnie, Erv, and Alicia were headed east on Interstate 44. The cabins at Wilson's Creek were cleaned out while Alicia packed her suitcase. They would need to go back to St. Louis to finish things up for Tom, since he had no family. They knew it would be a nightmare to jump through the hoops of red tape.

Bonnie knew it was possible that they wouldn't be able to do anything at all, but Tom was their friend. She knew she had to try. Mel and Alice were more than eager to watch Cujo for Bonnie. That dog would eat better than most people for the next few days.

"So, I took the cash I had in my apartment, but it isn't much," Alicia said. "Do we have a plan to get cash beyond the week?"

"We'll figure it out," Erv said. "Bonnie and I have a little saved up from a previous venture."

"I think we'll be fine," Bonnie said, thinking of the money she had gotten from the grain.

"I've never been to St. Louis."

"Really?" Erv asked, turning to look at Alicia in the back seat.

"Really."

"I think you'll like it. Quite a bit different than Springfield," Erv said, looking back out the windshield.

The interstate rose and fell with the Ozark mountains. The mostly undisturbed forest on either side of the highway offered breathtaking views. Alicia had actually never been more than an hour from Springfield, so she found herself staring out the window while the other two chatted in the front seat.

"What's the plan?" Erv asked.

"I think we should look for any sort of will or legal paperwork at Tom's apartment. We'll need to make arrangements for him, although I'm guessing it'll be a small service."

"I have a key. Actually, I still have some of my stuff there. I figured we'd be back in the apartment after coming to see you. Hadn't really thought about where I'm going to go."

"I bet the landlord will be happy to keep you on as a tenant. We should see about paying another month or whatever until this all shakes out," Bonnie said.

"I guess," Erv said. "It'll be weird not having Tom there, though."

Bonnie only nodded, feeling her breath catch at the thought of Tom being gone. She had done pretty well with handling the loss but found herself struggling in unexpected moments. Erv was not one to express his feelings openly. Once they made it through Rolla, they fell silent.

"Whoa," Alicia said, sitting up in her seat. "What is that?"

Bonnie glanced in her rearview to see where Alicia was looking and turned to look out the passenger window. An old green dump truck sat on top of a large platform made from boulders shaped into rough ovals. The truck marked the entrance to a large quarry.

"Oh, that old truck has been there forever," Bonnie said. "I thought it was pretty cool when I was a kid."

"Yeah, the truck's cool, but why is there a line of trailers down there? Looked kind of like those FEMA trailers from Hurricane Katrina."

"In the quarry?" Erv asked.

"I couldn't really see the quarry, just the row of trailers."

"Let's have a look," Bonnie said, and took the next exit. She turned right at her first chance and went back west along the frontage road that led to the quarry entrance. After winding along the road for about a mile and a half, they came to the freshly rocked entrance. A new sign stood along the east side of the drive.

"Quarry Village?" Erv said.

"That sounds weird," Alicia said. "Why would anyone want to live in an old quarry?"

Bonnie didn't comment but turned down the drive. They went along a curved driveway that went behind a grove of tall trees and then down into the quarry. A fifteen by fifteen metal shed stood on their right and a man in a brown uniform was seated inside a window in the southeast corner of the building. A ten foot long red and white bar blocked the entrance, but the guard raised it after a quick glance.

"Glad to see security is tight for whatever this place is," Erv said.

"Doesn't look like there is much to guard," Bonnie said, looking out at the crushed limestone road ahead of her.

A row of plain, tan trailers ran along either side. Another two rows of trailers were to their left on a separate road. If there had been a natural disaster, this would make sense, but things had been pretty calm in Missouri.

"What the heck is this?" Alicia asked.

"No clue," Erv said just before Bonnie brought the car to a stop.

A woman in a faded Cardinals tee and worn out jeans was sitting in a lawn chair next to one of the trailers. She had sunglasses on, but Bonnie could tell she was watching them. She got out and walked straight over to the woman.

"Are you a reporter?" the woman asked in a flat tone.

"Definitely not," Bonnie said. "What is this place?"

"I guess you aren't from around here," the woman said and picked up a blue plastic cup from the table next to her.

"Actually, I am, but I've been down around Springfield for the last few months. I lost my job up here and had to figure something out."

"Well, then you've missed the whole show. I figured it would have made the news down there, considering the governor was involved."

"My name is Bonnie, by the way. My friends in the car are Erv and Alicia. We are headed back to the city to handle some unexpected arrangements," she said, trying not to talk about Tom.

"I'm Esther," the woman said. "You want the long or short story?"

"Whichever you'd prefer," Bonnie said and glanced at the folding chairs leaning against the trailer.

"All right, well, you and your friends better grab those chairs. Oh, and you should move your car out of the middle of the road. Carlton is the guard working today and he gets weird sometimes about where people are parked."

"He didn't even question us on our way in."

"That sounds right," Esther said. "He doesn't care who he lets in but likes to treat the people who live here like second class citizens."

"That sucks," Bonnie said. "I'll be right back."

She went to the car and pulled it onto the little gravel patch that was supposed to serve as a driveway for Esther's trailer. Esther hadn't moved, other than to take another drink from her cup. Bonnie, Erv, and Alicia picked out chairs and created a half circle around Esther.

"So, this all started about two years ago when Gruesome got elected mayor of St. Louis."

"Gruesome?" Alicia asked.

"That's what we call her," Esther said with a grin. "Anyway, she thought that downtown needed to be improved in hopes of attracting more visitors and businesses. The streets are a wreck and there are a ton of dilapidated old buildings. Instead of working on that, she listened to some of her biggest donors and focused on a far less expensive task. She put the squeeze on homeless people and the shelters we called home most of the time."

"Isn't she a Democrat?" Erv asked. "I'd think that would put her on the other side of that argument."

"It sure seems like that'd be the case, but she even went after Barry Dice. I'll admit that the guy is a little off, but he has worked hard to protect the homeless."

"I think I've seen him on TV," Erv said. "It is amazing what you find on those antenna channels."

"After she tried closing him down, some guys that had been staying at Barry's place went over to Gruesome's house and threw rocks through some windows," Esther said. "Not a smart move, but hardly cause for what she did next."

"Which was?" Alicia asked.

"She arranged with some of her friends to purchase this quarry. Then, they bought all of these used trailers and moved them in. The utilities were done quickly, and you have to watch your step around the trenches if you leave your trailer, which they discourage. Finally, one of the friends who had bought this place set up a 501c3 charitable organization to house the homeless. The mayor was excited to say that she was curing homelessness in St. Louis, which is true, I guess. The thing is we are basically prisoners here and we have no way of trying to make money or better ourselves, but at least we aren't ruining the city."

"That has to be one of the worst things I've ever heard."

"Yeah, well, it won't last forever. The money will run out on this place and they'll probably just dump us out in the middle of nowhere. Anything to make sure we aren't a blight on St. Louis."

"Some of us could probably make it to another city and go back to our old way of life. Moving takes money though and we certainly don't have any. What it boils down to, is that we don't want to leave St Louis. We might be homeless, but it's still our home."

Bonnie nodded and looked at Alicia, then turned her gaze to Erv. His brow showed a deep furrow, and a huge frown stood where his smile normally would have been among his shaggy beard. He was looking along the road toward the office.

"I know a guy who would love to help with this down on Cherokee Street," Erv said.

"What guy?" Esther asked.

"Mark Frank."

Esther smiled, revealing pearly white teeth. She noticed Erv staring at her teeth.

"I brush regularly. Not much else to do out here."

"Crest?" Erv asked.

"Yep, but they only give us the original paste."

"I like mint better myself."

"If you two are done discussing oral hygiene, I think we can go," Bonnie said, interrupting their flirting.

"Alright, then," Esther said, her eyes still locked on Erv's.

"Yeah, let's go," he said.

"Ugh," Alicia said and walked to the car. "Esther, if you get in the back seat, I doubt the guard will even notice.

Minutes later, the guard raised the arm blocking the driveway after barely glancing up from his magazine. He might have tried to stop them, if he had known what they were about to do.

18

Bonnie dropped Esther and Erv off at Treffpunkt in South City. It was an old church that had been converted into a meeting space and had become a favorite of social activists in the city. Bonnie knew they had some work to do with taking care of Tom's business, but Erv was too distracted to be of any help. Alicia wanted to stay with Bonnie, so they went to Tom's apartment.

"Kinda weird seeing a church being used like that," Alicia said after Bonnie parked the car.

"You'll get used to it," Bonnie said. "There are a ton of empty churches in St. Louis, and small businesses are moving in. Coffee shops are a good fit, usually."

"I'll never complain about a good coffee shop."

"Yeah, and you won't find a Starbucks in a setting like that. Thank goodness," Bonnie said. "Let's go in."

She led the way from the car to the narrow door at the side of the deli. Bonnie had Tom's key, so she went in and up the stairs to the apartment on the left. She could feel the tears coming back as she put the key in the lock but took a deep breath to hold back the pain. Alicia gave her a soft pat on the shoulder.

Bonnie twisted the key, then the knob, and pushed the door open. It gave a brief squeak and stopped just short of the wall. The apartment was almost empty, and Bonnie felt bad for not realizing what Tom's life had been like before they lost their jobs. She hoped he had been happy with their adventure and that he had gotten some joy from it before he died.

"So, what are we looking for?" Alicia asked, not wanting to rush Bonnie.

"I'm sure there are some legal documents somewhere," Bonnie said, walking into the small space. "Probably a shoe box or something along those lines."

"Like that one?" Alicia asked after crossing toward the windows at the front of the apartment. A small box with the Amazon logo on the side was tucked behind a worn out end table with envelopes inside. The right end of each envelope was torn open and had words printed in thick permanent marker.

"Exactly what I expected from Tom," Bonnie said with a smile. "Looks simple enough."

"Yeah, especially since the second one has 'WILL' on it."

"This might be a quicker stop than expected," Bonnie said and pulled out the folder. The very first page was a handwritten note from Tom. She read it out loud. "Well, if you are reading this, then I guess I checked out. I hope I went out on a high note, but I guess it doesn't matter at this point. I don't have much in the way of finances, but I did make sure I wouldn't leave any bills behind. Please take this folder to Danielle Ledet. She's an attorney with an office on Arsenal and has all my instructions for taking care of things. I didn't want to leave anything to stress over for anyone. She will be donating all my stuff to Goodwill. If you want anything, you better grab it now. Please let Bonnie know I always thought of her as a daughter and Erv as a son. Tell them to take care of each other. See you on the other side! Tom."

Bonnie dropped into the single remaining chair and started crying. She had been holding it in as best as she could, but that dam had broken. Alicia knelt next to her and gave her a hug. They hadn't known each other long, but that didn't matter.

"Okay, enough of that," Bonnie said.

"Take all the time you need," Alicia said. "I don't think we're in a rush."

"I'm good," Bonnie said, wiping her eyes. "Let's find another box or two. I want all his pictures and anything that looks personal. There isn't much in here to donate anyway."

They found a plastic tub that had been flipped upside down to be used as a side table next to his bed. Bonnie took every picture and anything she could find that was handwritten. An old Bible that was inscribed with a note from Tom's grandma was on the shelf near the door, so she made sure it had a safe spot in the tub. She would have taken everything, but she knew she had nowhere to put it.

"Think he would care if I took this lamp?" Alicia asked from the living room, where she was studying a vintage lamp that looked like something from one of the old mansions in the central west end.

"All yours," Bonnie said, knowing he would be happy for Alicia to have it. "I think I've got everything I want. One last thing, though."

"What's that?" Alicia asked, while unplugging the lamp.

"He was a stickler than any visitor had to have something to drink."

"Sounds good to me."

"Looks like we have water, Pepsi, and a beer."

"I think we should leave the last beer," Alicia said. "I'll take a Pepsi though."

"That beer was probably for Erv. I think Tom liked the harder stuff when he did partake," Bonnie said. She handed a Pepsi to Alicia and took a bottle of water for herself.

Alicia carried her lamp and a set of coasters she found, while Bonnie took the tub of keepsakes. They loaded up the car and drove down the street to the lawyer Tom had mentioned. It was a quick process, and they were on their way back to where they had dropped off Erv and Esther. Bonnie kept the note from Tom and told Erv he would need to get his stuff from the apartment by the next day.

19

"Bonnie!" Erv said when they walked in the door at Treffpunkt. "You are not going to believe who is here."

Bonnie was still thinking about Tom and definitely not in the mood for Erv's games. She looked at him with a straight face and waited for him to continue. Esther was standing to his left talking to a couple of people. It was a little surprising to see a crowd of about fifty throughout the large room.

"They are having a planning meeting tonight and they brought in a caterer for the meal."

"Cool," Bonnie said.

"That's not the good part!" he said. "Come in the kitchen with me."

Erv was already on his way, so she followed. She couldn't guess who this person would be and didn't really care until she stepped through the double doors. The smiling face that greeted her was quite familiar.

"Bonnie!"

"Amber?"

"It's good to see you," Amber said and walked over to give her a hug. "Ryan is here, too. He's out back unloading a truck."

"I thought you guys were heading to Omaha."

"We did, but it turns out that working for family isn't all it's cracked up to be. I was reading a blog talking about the work some groups are doing here in St. Louis, so I did a little more research. Turns out there are quite a few little places that need catering work, but on a smaller scale than what most of the catering companies are willing to do."

"So, it's doing something you like for a good cause," Bonnie said. "Hard to beat that."

"Yeah, we're enjoying it. We've been here a week. Where's the rest of the crew?"

"Erv didn't tell you?"

"Tell me what?" Amber asked, looking out to the main room, where Erv had his arm around Esther's shoulders.

"Well, I'm not really up for telling a long story," Bonnie said, picking up a towel from the stainless steel counter to her right. "Erv and Tom and I decided to help out some people who were in a bind with a little help from some other friends. Things didn't go how we had planned, and Tom was shot. He's dead."

Amber stared at Bonnie for a long moment and then hugged her. They stood like that for a while, only separating when Ryan came back inside. He could see something wasn't right.

"What's wrong?" he asked.

"Tom was killed," Amber said.

"What?" Ryan said as his brow furrowed.

"He died for a good cause," a deep voice said from behind Ryan, and they all turned. No one was there. Bonnie knew who it was.

"Who said that?" Amber asked, leaning to look around some cabinets. She knew it wasn't Erv's voice.

"We are Legion," the voice said in a low, even tone.

"This is kind of freaking me out," Ryan said. "Is this some sort of trick?"

"Far from it," Bonnie said, still looking sad. "Legion would be the friend I mentioned before."

"Where is he?"

"That's where it gets a little complicated," Bonnie said, looking over at Alicia, who had started cutting vegetables for a soup. Old restaurant habits were hard to break. "Do you really want to know?"

Bonnie felt a slight reservation, thinking maybe Tom would be alive without Legion.

"That was not our fault," Legion said so that only Bonnie could hear.

"I know, but I can't go through that again," Bonnie thought.

"There is power in numbers, Bonnie. The more people you bring to the team, the more effective you will be."

"Fine," Bonnie said out loud.

"Who are you talking to?" Ryan asked.

"I am talking to Legion. They are an army of supernatural beings that work to help those in need."

"Oh, is that all?" Ryan asked. "Why can't we see them?"

"Ryan," Amber said, "I don't think you can see demons. That's what Legion is, right?"

"We are not a fan of that term. It is a name given to our kind by those in power, who want things to happen by their rules alone."

"So, we can hear them?"

"Yes. You can hear us," Legion said. "You just have to accept that you are hearing us."

"So, it's not a trick?"

"No," Bonnie said, feeling the stress build.

"And how exactly does a bodiless army help? Is it something like that final scene in Lord of the Rings?"

"Hollywood comes up with strange things," Legion said. "We work through the bodies of others."

"You possess people?" Amber asked, eyes wide open. She looked from Bonnie to Erv and then Alicia.

"Again," Legion said, "you have seen too many movies."

"Talk isn't going to get this done, and we need to get on with whatever is going to happen," Bonnie said, starting for the back door. "Come with me."

They stepped out into a small gravel lot and Bonnie picked up a rock the size of a large grape. She tossed it to Ryan, who caught it and looked back at her.

"Crush it."

"What?"

"Crush it. Turn it into powder."

"Have you lost your mind? It's a rock."

"I just want you to try," Bonnie said. Ryan squeezed it in his hand and then between both hands, getting little more than some dust off the rock and red spots on his palms. "Give it back to me."

Ryan handed it back to her and watched. Alicia had followed them out, wanting to see how Bonnie would handle this. She took a spot next to Amber, who was shaking a little.

"Watch," Bonnie said and took the rock between her thumb and forefinger of her right hand. She held her left hand, palm open, under the rock. She pinched and the rock splintered into a dozen pieces, falling to her palm. She squeezed with her left hand, then opened it to reveal a neat pile of powdered limestone.

"Whoa," Ryan said, staring at the powder, but not blinking. Bonnie dusted off her hand.

"Not everything requires brute force," Amber said.

"That's true," Alicia said, "but having an army to back up your plan never hurts. I know we don't know each other, but you gotta trust me on this one. I was in an abusive situation and knowing I could physically stand up to him gave me the strength to push him away."

Amber studied her, but then nodded.

"I get it," Amber said. "I'm just not sure about this whole possession thing. It goes against everything I've been taught my entire life."

"We are here to help, and we do our best to not take things too far. We have been around a long time, and some fights require different approaches than others."

"Bonnie, what happens if you don't want Legion in you anymore?"

"Then we go," Legion answered. "This is teamwork, so both sides have to want to be on the team."

"I'm in," Ryan said. "Show me how to break a rock like that."

Legion didn't say anything, but everyone saw Ryan stand up a little straighter. He took a deep breath and smiled. Amber frowned, still not sure about what she was watching.

"Ah, you are going to be fun," Legion said. "Never mind with the rock. That broken basketball rim needs to come down. Correct?"

"Yeah, the guy in charge of this place said it has been hanging like that for a long time," Ryan said. "They just haven't taken the time to remove it. The pole is rusted out and he's afraid a kid is going to get hurt."

"Pull it out," Legion said. Ryan smiled. He went to the pole and got a good grip. He pulled, but nothing happened. Ryan's face turned red, and then he stopped.

"I guess it's too much to do something like that," Ryan said.

"No, you simply must want it enough. You cannot do it on your own," Legion said. Bonnie crossed her arms, and a little smile formed at the corner of her lips, remembering the ways Legion had helped her.

"Alright, then," Ryan said and grabbed the pole again. "Can I get a little help, Legion?"

"Absolutely."

Ryan braced himself, squatted, and started to pull. The ground around the pole began to crumble as the concrete foundation around it appeared. Ryan wasn't even breathing hard as the four inch wide pole tipped over. He dropped it and looked back up at his audience.

"Wow," he said, grinning at Amber, who looked to be in shock.

20

"Hey! Can I have everyone's attention?" called a bald man from the front of the main room at Treffpunkt. "I hope everyone got enough to eat. I've been told there is still plenty left for seconds, if you want more. Amber and Ryan offered to take the leftovers to the church down the road after the meeting. On that note, I'd like to say a special thank you to Amber and her team for putting together this meal."

The group of about seventy offered a gracious applause, but soon fell silent again. Amber and the others who had worked on the meal were standing at the back of the room. Each offered a smile and a quick wave.

"Now, for those of you who haven't attended one of our meetings before, I'm Mark Frank. I'm not necessarily the leader, but I do volunteer to organize these get-togethers."

"No need to be humble!" called a man with shaggy brown hair standing along a side wall.

"Fine, fine," Mark said with a smile. "Anyway, we have been hoping to put together a march that will show our displeasure with the way city hall is handling our homeless citizens. If you are here, then I'm sure you are aware of how hard the mayor is working to 'fix' the issue in her own despicable way. It's time to let the people of St. Louis and beyond really know what is happening because the mayor's friends are doing a great job of keeping things out of the news."

"What's the plan?" asked a woman from a table near the front.

"Well, Kate, we are going to hear from someone close to the situation. Then, I'm open to suggestions. Esther, can you come on up?"

Esther had been sitting next to Erv at a folding table about half way back on the right. Bonnie and Alicia were sitting across from her. They offered a supportive smile as she took a deep breath and started toward the front.

"Hello," she said when she got to the microphone. "I'm really bad at public speaking, and I'm doing my best not to puke right now."

"You got this!" Erv yelled and a wave of laughter went across the room. Erv blushed when he realized people were staring at him. Bonnie rolled her eyes.

"Thanks, Erv," Esther said. "So, I'm sure many of you have heard of Quarry Village. The plan sounds great on paper, but I can assure you, as a resident, that it is horrid. If we speak out, then we are called ungrateful because we have a place to live and a basic supply of food. When we were on the street, those things were hard to come by. The problem comes with the fact that we are not allowed to leave, and this is enforced by guards at the entrance to the quarry. The trailers we live in are leftovers from some FEMA project. They leak and are too hot to be in when the sun is up most days. Again, I know it sounds like complaining, but I promise it is as bad as it sounds. When we were able to go to a shelter, at least we still had freedom. The food supplies they bring us are all canned, and there is never anything fresh. Even people driving through the city would offer fresh fruit sometimes. We are basically in a prison because we are homeless. The kids are bussed out to school but are still treated as homeless. Some of the residents at the quarry are content, but most would rather have their old life back. Many would rather have a temporary place to stay and some opportunities to work, which is something the mayor has not been willing to listen to. We don't want to be homeless, but without a home or any sort of money, it is a steep climb. I know most of us would be willing to march, if we could get out of the quarry. I'm only able to be here because Erv and his friends acted like I went into the quarry with them. There is no way the guard would have let me out otherwise. We are willing to march to increase the numbers, but we won't be able to offer anything to defray costs."

"Costs shouldn't be an issue," Mark said, joining her at the mic. "We just need a big enough crowd to make it newsworthy. I think we can organize something to spring those who are willing from the quarry, and I think most people here are ready to march. Right?"

Cheers erupted from the group. There were smiles of joy and determination on most faces. It was clear the march was going to happen.

"Thank you, Esther," Mark said, and she went back to her table. "Now, we have been told that certain groups will try to stop us and that the mayor's friends have employed counter-protestors to make our march hard to execute. We aren't looking for a fight, but we will not back down."

"We have that covered," called a confident voice from somewhere near the back. Most people turned to see who had said it, but no one could figure it out. "You gather the people, and we will make sure the march happens."

"Legion," Bonnie said softly.

"It is what we do," Legion replied so only she could hear.

"Fine, but how are you going to explain this to a crowd?"

"You think this is the first time?"

Bonnie sat back, thinking that Legion was right and that thousands of years of experience certainly would be hard to beat in a debate.

"We are Legion," the voice said again. "Many of you look confused, so let us try this a different way. Bonnie, would you mind?"

Bonnie sighed and stood up. She walked to the front of the room but did not go to the microphone. She stopped between two tables in the front row and turned to face everyone.

"Go ahead," she said, her voice barely carrying to the back of the room.

"As we said," the voice continued, now broadcasting from Bonnie, using her voice. Only now her voice was strong and loud, easily heard by anyone who cared to listen. "We are Legion. We are here to help and would love nothing more than to provide the muscle that this group needs."

"What is going on?" Mark asked, looking bewildered and uneasy.

"Listen to us," Legion continued. "We are not people, but instead a supernatural type of help, if you can grasp that."

People began to mumble, questioning those around them. Bonnie waited, thinking Legion must have a plan. The mumbles grew, and people stood up.

"Sit down, please," Legion said, but some did not. "We said *sit*!"

Everyone went back into their seats, and the room fell silent.

"Now, it can be confusing, and few of you know what is going on. Several here have already accepted our help. As more of you let us in, the level of our effectiveness grows."

"Let us in?" Kate asked, in an uncertain voice. "Are you demons or ghosts or something?"

"We get that a lot and, yes, that is a good enough way to describe us. The key is that we are not evil, but instead working to help those in need. Oftentimes, that puts us at odds with those in positions of authority. Then, we earn a negative name, but that is okay."

"I'm a little freaked out, right now," Kate said.

"We hear that a lot, too. Just know that we want to help, and we certainly can help. Bonnie, here, has enjoyed our help," Legion said before pointing at others around the room using Bonnie's body. "Erv, Alicia, and Ryan have accepted our help, and I think they are happy with that decision."

"I know I certainly am!" Alicia said, standing from her seat. "Legion helped me get rid of a disgusting predator. I've never felt better."

"What exactly do you need from us?" Mark asked, returning to the microphone. Bonnie turned to look at him.

"A willingness to let us help," Legion said. "All you have to do is let us in."

"And you'll help us with the march?"

"Definitely."

"I'll give it a shot," Mark said and took a half step back as if a sudden gust of wind had hit him. His chin dropped to his chest, and he stood still for a moment. "Wow."

He looked back out at the crowd and smiled, raising his arms.

"This feels amazing," Mark said. "I think the mayor is in for a surprise."

21

"Hello?"

"Michelle? This is Bonnie."

"Oh, hey Bonnie! How are you?"

"Busy is a good word, I guess," Bonnie said and let a pause grow. "You want to come to St Louis and help us out?"

"What's wrong?"

"A lot has happened since I saw you, but we are planning a march on city hall here. The mayor shipped all the homeless people to a camp of sorts, and we just found out she wants to demolish any building in the poor part of the city that is considered vacant."

"Wow," Michelle said. "So, who is with you? I guess Tom and Erv are there? What about Tiny and Giant?"

"Erv is here, along with Amber and Ryan. Tom, well, he's dead."

"What?" Michelle said and her voice caught. "How?"

"We were helping out with a situation down in Springfield, and a crooked lawyer shot him."

"When is the march?"

"Day after tomorrow," Bonnie said, taking a seat in a comfortable blue chair in her room at the Red Lion Hotel. She looked around the room and then up at the clear blue sky over St. Louis. "Can you come?"

"I'm already in St. Louis. I'm doing promotions at the Muny."

"Well, that works out well," Bonnie said.

"Yep, I have to work tonight, but I'll meet you for coffee in the morning if you want."

"That sounds good. I think we are heading out to meet with the homeless tomorrow around lunch time. You are welcome to join. I'm going to call Giant next."

"Okay, cool," Michelle said. "I'll meet you at Catalyst Coffee Bar at eight. I've got a couple friends who might want to join, if that's okay."

"The more the merrier," Bonnie said. "See you there."

Bonnie put her phone on the side table and leaned back in the chair. She was exhausted and wanted a nap in the worst way. She hadn't been able to sleep more than an hour or two at a time since Tom was killed. She knew there was work to be done but felt like she was going through the motions instead of really feeling them. She had read articles on grief, but nothing made her feel better.

"I just want to sleep," she said.

A gentle hum, like an orchestra full of cellos, began. She did not open her eyes, but wondered where the soothing sound was coming from. She focused on it and felt the tightness in her shoulders begin to relax.

"Sleep now," Legion said, and the humming continued. She realized it was Legion's many voices in perfect harmony, and consciousness left her.

"Baby shark. Do do do, do do do do do," sang her cell phone, and she groaned. "Baby shark. Do do…"

"Yeah," she said after swiping at the green symbol on her phone.

"Did I wake you up?"

"Yes, Erv. I haven't slept well in days and finally fell asleep a couple minutes ago."

"Oh, sorry about that. I was hoping to catch you before you went to bed."

"Bed? It's only a little after 4," Bonnie said and turned to look at the digital clock on the small table between the beds. It read 9:50.

"I think you must've gotten a little rest after all," Erv said, and Bonnie knew he was smirking. "I'll let you get back to sleep, but I wanted to let you know that I talked to Giant a little bit ago. They're on a bus headed for St. Louis. Apparently, they had a feeling that they should come up."

"That's pretty convenient," Bonnie said.

"Convenient is not the word you are looking for," Legion said. "We thought you could use a little more help, so we reached out. A bit of a stretch for us, but it worked."

"Erv, I'm meeting Michelle at Catalyst Coffee tomorrow at eight. Can you bring Esther and Alicia and meet up with us? I'll call Giant and tell them they can crash at my hotel room since the bus station is right here. Then, we can all go out to the quarry."

"You always have a plan," Erv said. "I think I'll start calling you Hannibal."

"Like the guy from Silence of the Lambs?"

"No," Erv said. "Colonel John 'Hannibal' Smith of the A-Team, of course."

"I think I saw an episode of that once. Boy George was in it."

"I remember that one. You are totally missing out. Anyway, yeah, I'll be at Catalyst in the morning. Rest up. I think you're going to need it."

"Probably so," Bonnie said and ended the call.

"Your team is almost all back together," Legion said. "The next forty-eight hours are going to be big for you."

"Like it or not, huh."

"You can walk away anytime. Just say the word. We've been pretty honest about how our agreement works."

"I'm exhausted. These last few months have been hard. I never bargained for anything like this."

"When one person does something for another person it starts a chain reaction. You have helped several people, even if you do not realize it. They have started helping others, so the reaction is getting big. Figure in the effect you are going to have on thousands of people in the next couple days and you will be on your way to accomplishing more than you ever imagined."

"It all sounds good, but at what cost? I've already lost the only person I had left that was family to me."

"Doing the right thing is not always easy, and you know you have a family, even if they are not the traditional kind."

"What about you?"

"Well, we are more like a support team, not family."

Bonnie thought about her crew and knew Legion was right. She was reluctant to think of them that way in case something bad happened, but she had to accept she couldn't control everything.

"You need more rest," Legion said. "Tomorrow is going to be a long day."

"Okay, let me call Giant and Amber before I fall asleep. Will you do that humming thing again?"

"Sure."

22

Bonnie, Giant, and Tiny walked into Catalyst about five minutes before 8 the next morning. The barista smiled but looked a little nervous when Tiny got to the counter.

"Welcome to Catalyst. I'm Corbin. What can I make for you?"

"We are meeting some people," Bonnie said. "Should be maybe three or four?"

"Well, there is a group of ten back in the gallery at our big table. I think everyone else is pretty much solo."

"Ten?" Bonnie said, wondering if Michelle had understated how many people were interested.

"I'll go see if it's them," Giant said, but stopped when he saw Michelle come around the corner. "Hey!"

"Giant!" she said and rushed over to give him a hug. Then, she looked up at Tiny, who had a playful grin on his face. "Of course, you get a hug too, big guy."

"It's like a homecoming," Bonnie said, enjoying the happiness in the room and hugging Michelle. "We'll get our drinks and come back to the table. Today is going to be a good day."

"I brought some friends!"

"That's what Corbin said."

"Who?"

"That's me," the barista said with a little wave.

"Oh, sorry."

"No worries."

"Okay," Bonnie said. "Salted caramel latte for me."

"We will take large black coffees," Giant said. "How much are refills?"

"Fifty cents," Corbin said, "but you can get a bottomless cup for a dollar extra."

"Sold!" Giant said. "And look what the cat has dragged in."

Erv, Alicia, Esther, Amber, and Ryan walked in the front door. The energy in the room was palpable. Everyone was excited for the reunion.

"The gang is all here," Legion said. Michelle, Tiny, and Giant got confused looks on their faces. Bonnie gave a halfhearted smile in reply. "Time for a chat?"

"Um. What?" Michelle asked.

"Let's head back to your table and fill you in," Bonnie said. "These four are up to speed, so they can get their drinks."

"Caramel Salted Latte for Bonnie and two black coffees, bottomless, for the gentlemen."

"It's been a while since anyone referred to us as gentlemen, Tiny," Giant said, and Tiny gave a short laugh.

Michelle's friends were talking when Bonnie and the others came around the corner. The big table, as it had been described, still had empty seats and the smaller eight-person table next to it was vacant. Bonnie took a long drink from her latte and then sighed.

"Okay," she said. "Today is going to be a big day for us and hopefully the homeless people of the city. Our goal is to bring attention to this issue and try to solve it with support within the city instead of hiding the people in an old quarry. They will never get the chance to improve their situation, find work, or stay in touch with family if they are way out in the middle of nowhere in a camp that has its entrance guarded twenty-four hours a day. To be clear, the guard is there to keep the people in, no matter what the mayor and her friends have said."

"What are we going to do about it?" asked one of Michelle's friends. "I mean, what *can* we do?"

"We are going to lead a march of sorts that will take those people out of the camp and straight to the steps of city hall," Bonnie said. "There will probably be about fifty people from South City joining us, along with any of you that want to come along."

Michelle's friends were on board, as were the rest of Bonnie's friends. There was a pause that stretched across several long seconds, but it was broken by a strong voice.

"There is one major detail that Bonnie is leaving out."

"There's that voice again!" Michelle said. "Who said that?"

"We are Legion," the voice said. "We are here to help with this endeavor."

"Ok," Bonnie said. "I got in a bind a couple months ago and accepted help from something I didn't understand. I can't imagine what would have happened to me without help from Legion, but I also wonder if Tom would still be here. To put it bluntly, Legion is a supernatural army that provides the support we've needed in a couple situations and that we are probably going to need again on this march."

"We are going to need an army of demons to help us?" Michelle asked.

"Not a big fan of the demon label," Legion said. "We are here to help. If you do not want the help, that is fine. If you want help now and decide later that you do not, then off we go. Even Bonnie could do that, but she has not yet."

"So, Bonnie, what you're telling us, is that you're possessed?" Giant said.

"Something like that, I guess."

"Yes!" Ryan said. "So am I. Erv and Alicia, too. Man, I pulled a basketball pole complete with its concrete footing right out of the ground. I didn't even have to try, really."

"What about you, Amber?" Michelle asked.

"Nope, not me. Still kinda weirds me out, but so far, I'm dealing with it. It boils down to the fact that we are a team and Legion is part of it. I think the power could be addictive, but having the ability to stop at any time has me almost ready to jump in."

"What do you think, Tiny? Are we all in?" Giant said. Tiny stared at him for a moment and then looked at Bonnie.

"Yes," the big man said, and then his head bowed. He gripped the edge of the metal table and held himself steady. When he relaxed and looked up again, his fingers had been permanently imprinted into the table.

"That was intense," Michelle said. "Tiny, you were already the biggest, strongest guy I've ever met. Now, you are unstoppable, I think."

He smiled, looked at Giant, and then picked up his coffee cup like someone might pick up a fragile glass sculpture. He took a drink and then looked up to see everyone staring at him. He raised his eyebrows, and Giant started laughing.

"Well, then I guess I'm in, too," Michelle said, and that's all it took. Michelle's friends were right behind her, and even Amber joined the group before they left the coffee shop.

23

Bonnie brought her car to a stop about fifty feet before the entrance to the quarry. One of Michelle's friends was right behind her in a van. Together they had seventeen people packed in their vehicles and were prepared for the day. They got out, retrieved their backpacks from the rear of the van, and waited for Bonnie's instructions.

"We are going to walk in from here," she said. "Esther said there is usually only one guard on duty, so I don't foresee that being a problem. Alicia and Amber, I need you to take both vehicles to Target over on Highway 30. We will march from here to there and stop for the night. You two will be in charge of stocking up on water and food for the next day and a half. Fill up the van and my car if possible. There is an envelope in my glovebox that should get what we need. The rest of us will go into the quarry under the guise of people coming in to help around the camp. I'll talk to the guard. Once we are in, pair off and start knocking on doors. We need to be walking out of here in an hour. Got it?"

Everyone gave their assent.

"We will see you a bit," Amber said and turned to Ryan. "Be careful."

"We'll be fine," he said. "Legion has our back."

"Okay," she said and kissed him.

"Do I get a kiss, too?" Erv asked, puckering his lips.

Esther elbowed him in the ribs.

"I'm sure Esther will hook you up," Amber said and got in Bonnie's car.

"Let's go," Bonnie said and started along the driveway into the quarry.

The other fourteen were right with her, but it was clear that Bonnie was the leader.

"You will be fine," Legion said to her. "We are not going to allow this to go poorly. You have a good plan."

"Every plan has a flaw, Legion."

"Rely on your team, and you will succeed."

Bonnie kept walking, trying to focus on the task ahead of her. They went around the curve and up over a little rise before descending into the quarry for the last time. The guard was inside the office, but the arm was down across the road. He came out when he saw them coming down the hill.

"What can I do for you all?" the guard said. He was holding a cup of coffee and munching on a doughnut. He was not interested in whatever they were doing but had to do his job.

"We are just here to offer a little help to residents," Bonnie said with a smile. "Our bus driver didn't think he could get turned around down here, so we just walked in."

"Yeah, it can get a little tight down here for a big vehicle," the guard said and tore off another bite of doughnut. "I didn't have a message about any workers coming in today, but I don't feel like messing with it. You look harmless, so just go on in and do whatever it is you are here to do. How many of you are there?"

"Fifteen," Bonnie said.

"Good. Make sure you check all fifteen out before sundown. It is a sort of curfew thing we have. For the safety of our residents, of course."

"Oh, of course," Bonnie said. "We will be on our way well before sunset."

"Great!" the guard said and went back inside. Bonnie's team walked around the red and white striped arm and into the quarry.

"Okay, everyone needs their best shoes, and a blanket. If they have a water bottle, they should bring it. Move quickly and meet at Esther's trailer, it's number 211, in an hour. Everyone take a partner. Erv, will you take one for the team and work with Esther?"

"You don't have to ask me twice!" he said and smiled at her. The others split off into pairs.

Most of the people were receptive to what Bonnie's team had in mind. Some were unable to walk, but offered up what they could in support of the others. After only twenty minutes, the eight teams had become twenty and word spread quickly that they were on the move. A total of nearly two hundred met at Esther's trailer a short while later. Bonnie was glad the guard couldn't see them from his window. No advanced warning for him made her feel more at ease.

"What next?" Giant said as the last few stragglers joined the crowd. "Want me to quiet them down? I have a big voice."

"I have it under control," Legion said, and Bonnie's team waited as the murmuring grew louder.

"Be still," Legion said in a low voice, but one that all those in the crowd could hear. Silence fell at once. Bonnie stepped up onto Esther's porch and looked at the group. She smiled, although her face showed great concern for them.

"I'm going to lead us out of here," she said. "We are going to walk to the gate and up out of this place. These two guys are Tiny and Giant. They are going to talk to the guard for us on the way by. Once we are out, we will walk along Antire Road to Target and collect supplies that will be waiting for us. Tomorrow morning, we will begin the march into the city. I'm not sure what awaits us along the way, but I'm sure there will be resistance once they figure out what is going on. Be strong, keep your head up, and keep walking. Everyone ready?"

"Yeah!" the crowd cheered.

"Good! Now, let's go. Tiny, will you lead the way to the gate?"

Tiny nodded, turned, and started along the road back to the office. Hundreds of footfalls sounded like a heavy truck creeping along the gravel road. They made the turn onto the entrance road about fifty yards from the guard's office. He came out as soon as he saw them and watched them close to about twenty feet from the arm before stopping.

"Stop there!" he said, although they already had. "The residents have to sign out with a sponsor and have transportation. No one can leave on foot."

"We won't be signing out today," Esther said from the left end of the front row.

"Those are the rules!" he yelled back. The crowd stared back at him and waited. "You have to check out one at a time, too. So, go back to your homes and come up one at a time."

"We are all leaving together," Legion said. "We are Legion."

"We are Legion!" the group yelled, and Tiny rushed forward.

The guard reached for his pistol. Tiny, with the help of Legion, was there before the guard could unclip his weapon. The big man ripped the gun out of the holster, nearly tearing the belt from the guard's waist. He looked at it for a moment, cocked his head to the side, and squeezed the barrel flat. Then, he reached back like he was going to throw a fastball and launched the gun far beyond the rim of the quarry. It was still sailing when the crowd lost sight of it.

The guard looked back at Tiny and punched him in the stomach. He frowned with disapproval, although the punch itself had little effect on him. The guard realized this and stumbled back toward the building. Tiny reached out and grabbed him by the front of his blue button-down shirt. He lifted him about two feet off the ground and locked eyes with him.

"I'm sorry. I'm sorry!" the guard yelled. "I'm just doing my job. Don't hurt me!"

"Now he begs," Giant said and walked over to Tiny. He reached up and took the cell phone from the man's belt and flipped open the case. Giant smirked and squeezed it, crushing the phone into a wad of plastic and wires. He tossed it near the foundation of the office and gave the guard a smile.

"Just don't hurt me! I have kids! I have a family!"

"The people you work for don't care about that. They pulled these people away from their lives to try to make more money."

After a long pause, Bonnie said, "We aren't going to hurt anyone. We are going to walk out of here, and you aren't going to get in our way. What you do after we leave is up to you, but we are leaving."

"O-Okay," the guard said, and Tiny tossed him onto the roof of the office.

He landed with a thud. The impact knocked the wind from his lungs. He somehow avoided panicking, caught his breath, and scrambled to the peak of the roof. Once there, he looked back at the crowd. They could all see him shaking as if the temperature had just dropped fifty degrees.

"This is going to end badly for all of you! When I get down, I'm going to call the mayor!"

"You do that," Bonnie said. "She needs to know we are coming."

Several of the quarry residents rushed toward the red and white striped arm, took hold, and snapped it off at its base. They cheered and tossed it into the landscaping next to the office. It was a symbol of the restrictions they had been living under and they had removed it with little effort. Their confidence grew as they started up the hill. The guard did nothing besides watch them go.

24

The group filled the width of the driveway like a river finding its banks and flowed out onto the frontage road. Bonnie was pleased that they were on their way, but still had concerns about the length of the walk. They were a long way from downtown and she hoped these people would be able to do it. She worried that the group would dwindle to nothing before they got to City Hall.

The plan was to turn onto Antire Road and make that four plus mile hike before stopping. That would still leave over twenty miles. She was deep in thought, but a blaring horn sounded behind them brought her out of her trance.

"Get to the side of the road!" a man yelled from the back. The horn sounded again, and five buses pulled up alongside them. Mark, the leader of the group at Treffpunkt, was driving the first one.

He threw open the door when he was even with Bonnie.

"You all need a ride?"

Bonnie nodded and climbed aboard. The rest of the group followed suit, nearly filling all five buses.

"I've got a couple people waiting for us at the Target near Antire and Highway 30. We're going to need to go there," Bonnie said.

"Sure thing," Mark said before he glanced in the rearview to see that everyone had found a seat. "Then on to Minnie Ha Ha Park!"

"Wait, what?" Bonnie said, leaning forward from the seat behind the driver, looking at Mark in the mirror.

"Yeah, we've got a little surprise set up for you and the group."

"What is it?"

"Um, if I tell you, it won't be a surprise."

"I'm not four, Mark."

"Oh, I know, but you're going to have to wait for this one. Besides, Target is right up here. Just relax."

Bonnie stared at him, and then flopped back against the seat. She closed her eyes and tried to relax, but she was a planner and not knowing what was happening stressed her out.

Minutes later, they pulled into the Target parking lot. Bonnie spotted the van and her car along the east side of the lot. Alicia was waving as the buses pulled up.

Bonnie stood up and looked back at the people on her bus, "We have water and snacks for everyone at the van. The plan is to find a good spot to regroup and plan tomorrow's march. It sounds like some of our friends from South City have helped us out there. For now, grab a water and something to eat. We'll get back on the buses before long. Giant, will you go to the second bus and let them know?"

"Sure thing," Giant said and went down the stairs. The first bus was empty before too long and Bonnie had moved to the third bus. It seemed like a lot of people to tend to, but the whole group was refreshed within twenty minutes. Mark honked the horn on his bus.

"All aboard!" he yelled out the driver's window. People looked at Bonnie, who started toward the first bus. Again, she felt anxious about not knowing what was next, but she had to trust the help.

"It is a good plan," Legion said, but only Bonnie could hear.

"Yeah?"

"We were in on it. Do not forget the Treffpunkt group accepted our help."

"So, wait, you could be with us at the quarry and in the city?"

"Obviously. Can you and Alicia be two different places?"

"Well, yes."

"Okay, there are thousands of us," Legion said. "Whether we are in one body or many, we are still Legion."

"Got it," Bonnie said and looked out the window as the bus cruised along Highway 30. A shopping center on a stone bluff with a waterfall was to her right as they passed through Fenton. She thought about the homeless people and wondered if they could have even made this walk.

"They would have been fine," Legion said. "Most of them are willing to accept a little help from some friends."

Bonnie didn't reply. She watched the old part of Fenton slip by and then they went up over the Meramec River. She knew the park was to the right, but the trees were dense, so she couldn't see whatever Mark had set up. Just before the eastern boundary she saw a group of maybe fifty people on the soccer field.

The line of buses continued east another few hundred yards and then turned right and right again to head back toward the park. When they pulled into the main parking lot, Bonnie's eyes widened.

Six more buses of various sizes were in the soccer field parking lot. Hundreds of people were milling around, and some were starting to set up tents across the field. The smell of grilled food filled the air and provided a welcome greeting for Bonnie's group.

Bonnie saw one tent with a rainbow flag flying over it, another with a banner from St. Louis Interfaith, and yet another from the American Legion.

"I'm not sure how many Legions we can handle," she thought.

"Take all you can get," Legion told her.

"There are more people coming," Mark said. "I think we have about two hundred from our outreach at Treffpunkt. A couple of the universities have students coming in the morning to march. I think all three major TV stations have committed."

"And we are the first on the scene," said a woman in a moss green dress that was what most would call shabby chic. The combination of dress and accessories, plus a perfectly messy hairdo, was outstanding. "I'm Sonja with the Riverfront Times."

"Hi, I'm Bonnie. This is Mark."

"Ah, Bonnie, the one and only."

"Don't give me too much credit. It takes a team to make this work."

"Right," Sonja said, flipping open a small notepad. "Let's see. Erv, Alicia, Michelle, Giant, Tiny, Esther, and Mark here."

"That's a good start."

"And you all call yourself Legion?"

"Not exactly."

"My source said that there was something to do with your group and someone or a group called Legion."

"Yes, but it is complicated, and I'd rather focus on what we are doing here."

"Fair enough, so why are you doing it?"

"I would never want to be trapped in a camp like that. It might look good on the surface, but the real purpose is heinous at best. The mayor and her donors are out to make a buck, not really make the city better. People need to unite under a common cause to get things done for the betterment of all."

"Well said. I got similar sentiments from the LGBTQ leaders and a couple representatives from the American Legion. I'm sure you saw them. The Interfaith group is planning on drawing a lot of people."

"Great," Bonnie said. "The more the merrier!"

"I'll let you talk to your team, but I'll be around for a bit. I'd like to hear more about the Legion aspect of this movement."

"We are Legion," a soft and firm voice said. Sonja looked up at Mark and Bonnie.

"You are Legion?"

"No."

"But you said…"

"I didn't, but I think if you ask around you might get a better answer than what I can offer."

"Count on it," Sonja said. "I'm truly intrigued now."

Bonnie found the rest of her crew standing outside a blue, domed tent near the midfield line. They had found some beverages that were apparently donated by another group she hadn't heard from yet. Erv handed her a brown bottle, and they clinked the necks together. The music started somewhere down near the south goal. The atmosphere relaxed. Bonnie felt at ease, but then she noticed three black SUVs along the road leading to the park.

"I don't think they are here in support," she said, gesturing with her bottle.

"Probably not," Michelle said, "but all of these people are!"

"Let's enjoy the moment and prepare for a big day tomorrow," Amber said with a smile. "I know I smelled brats earlier."

"Yeah," Ryan said, "I'm hungry all of a sudden."

"Me too," Tiny said, and they all turned to look at him. He shrugged.

"You're always hungry, Ryan," Amber said. "Let's eat!"

The team drifted over toward the smell of brats, burgers, and hot dogs. They saw dozens of quarry residents smiling and enjoying themselves. Bonnie was pleased and thought that they deserved this at the very least.

25

"Wake up, Bonnie!" Michelle called. "The sun's up, and today is a big day. Another one of Mark's friends is here. He owns a coffee roasting company, and this stuff is good! There is also a breakfast burrito food truck out here. Some news people are here, too."

"Yeah, okay," Bonnie said, rubbing her eyes and blinking up at the roof of her tent. She had ended up in a small red tent with a sleeping bag that would have kept her warm in the arctic. It felt like she had gotten three or four hours of sleep, but it was probably more. A quick flip of her hair was the best anyone was going to get.

"That's her," said a woman in a perfectly pressed skirt and blouse.

She was holding a microphone, and a man with a camera on his shoulder was walking just behind her. Three other reporters, each with a cameraman, were close behind. Channels 2, 4, 5, and 11 were present and accounted for. Bonnie began to think she should avoid the interview.

"I will handle this," Legion said.

Tiny strode in from behind a tent to Bonnie's right. Giant followed at his left.

"Ladies and gentlemen," Tiny said in a calm, yet powerful, voice that Bonnie had never heard. "Bonnie will be available for interviews in a little while. For now, I will be happy to answer any questions you might have. Today is going to be a historic day for this city, and she has some last minute planning to do."

Giant looked at Bonnie, raised his eyebrows, and gestured toward the Stringbean Coffee truck. She realized she had a window to slip away, and she was off. For the first time in a while, she was truly happy to have Legion act on her behalf.

A twenty ounce cup of Robert's Roast and a short visit to the park's bath house left her feeling much better. Her breakfast burrito was delicious. Amber, Michelle, and Ryan had enlisted the help of several other people who had come to march to hand out bottles of water. It was clear that things were about to get started.

"It will be fine," Legion said to Bonnie.

"I hope so."

"Believe it!"

"Ok, then, that makes it all better," she said with a little sarcasm. "I do appreciate you redirecting those reporters earlier."

"Glad to help. That is what we do."

Bonnie took an extra bottle of water and started toward the south end of the parking lot. She wished that she could have brought Cujo but was sure her dog was enjoying his time with Mel and Alice.

"Is it go time?" Erv asked as she walked by.

"It is."

Erv started calling for everyone to get to the south end of the parking lot, and the word spread through the crowd. Minutes later, the flow of the crowd carried them out onto the highway. The march was officially underway. A crew was selected to stay behind to pack up, but about six hundred were moving toward city hall.

"Check this out!" one of the college students near the front of the group called out. "#marchforstlouis is trending on pretty much everything. Anyone know which way we are going?"

"We are going up Gravois," someone else answered. "I'll put it out there."

"I will, too!"

Bonnie continued on past them and climbed in the back of a pickup truck. She turned to look at the crowd and saw that they were slowly making their way in her direction. Erv handed her a bullhorn and she turned it on.

"Thank you all for coming out in support today," she
said. "We are going to have an impact, whether the mayor
likes it or not."

"Yeah!" the crowd cheered.

"We need everyone to remain safe during this march,
so please stay together and out of traffic! Hopefully we don't
meet too much resistance, but we will push through no
matter what."

The crowd cheered again and started stomping their
feet as they went by. Bonnie's attention was drawn to the
three SUVs on Old Gravois Road when their headlights
came to life. A bus bearing the American Legion logo rolled
past them and stopped at the entrance to the soccer parking
lot. A man in his dress Marine uniform exited the bus and
walked straight to Bonnie.

"Ma'am," he said. "I am Staff Sergeant Carlos Ford,
retired. We have twenty retired marines ready to march with
your group today, especially to support those veterans who
have been left homeless."

"Thank you," Bonnie said.

"It is our pleasure. We would also like to follow the
group with our bus to provide a place for walkers to rest
along the way and provide a blockade against anyone
driving up the rear of the group."

"Again, thank you. That would be great."

Ford turned around and twirled his hand in the air.
Nineteen more men in uniform exited the bus and lined up
along either side of Gravois Road. Several of the residents
of the quarry, some wearing Vietnam Veteran hats, stopped
to shake hands with the men. Bonnie's left shoelace had
come loose, so she tightened it up, and started east.

"Here we go," she said. Erv, Alicia, Esther, Michelle,
Ryan, Amber, Tiny, and Giant fell in with her. They were
smiling, but Bonnie was still nervous about how the march
would go. As she went by the SUVs, one window rolled
down six inches and a man wearing black shades stared out

at her. That was the only sign of resistance they saw for a while, since the SUVs would race past them about ten minutes later on Highway 30.

"Get off the road!" a passenger in a silver Jeep yelled as they raced by a little too close to the group. Bonnie and her friends were making sure everyone stayed on the shoulder, but that didn't seem to be good enough for some of the drivers.

"Crossing the interstate is going to be interesting," Erv said as he sped up to catch Bonnie. "Drivers are going to be blocked from getting on 270."

"So be it," she said and kept walking. Erv smiled at her resolve and dropped back to his position.

As the marchers approached the overpass, another group of about fifty started their way from a commuter parking lot. Bonnie was concerned for a moment, but then saw that two of them had signs that had #marchforstlouis on them. Most drivers were patient with the marchers, and they were soon past the interstate.

They marched past Lindbergh Boulevard and Grant's Farm. They were able to have lunch in the parking lot of the Grant's View library before continuing into Affton. The pace was a little slower than Bonnie had hoped, but the crowd had grown to over a thousand. She was getting reports that hundreds more were planning to join them later in the day. The American Legion bus was over half full because two dozen marchers simply couldn't keep going.

A little after three, a St. Louis County Police cruiser pulled up alongside the front of the crowd with two others flanking the group.

"Are you the organizer?" a female officer in the passenger seat asked Bonnie, who was still keeping a good pace in the lead.

"I'm one of them, yes," she said without slowing down. "We aren't breaking any laws."

"That could be debated, but that's not why we are here," the officer said. "I'm Officer Kizer and we are concerned about the safety of your group once rush hour starts here in the next hour. Gravois can get a little crazy."

"Traffic should be going the other way," Bonnie said. "I'm sure there aren't that many people going toward the city."

"You're right, but there are still quite a few and you are essentially blocking one of the two lanes. What is your destination exactly? We heard downtown."

"We are marching to city hall. We are going to talk to the mayor about her policies."

"That seems like a tough battle," Kizer said. "Good luck though."

"Thanks."

"Anyway, if you turn around, you can make it back to Grant's Trail and safely off the road."

"The bike path? There are a thousand of us at least. I think I have a better plan."

"What is it?"

"I know a good spot just across the River Des Peres that would put us within St. Louis city limits for the evening."

"I suppose you could make that in under an hour. We can help keep traffic to one lane until city limits."

"That would be appreciated. Tomorrow will be another story, though. We intend to start marching early."

"I'll reach out to some city officers I know and see what we can figure out."

"Thank you," Bonnie said. "My name is Bonnie Rose, by the way."

"Well, stay safe, Ms. Rose."

The car dropped back a bit but kept its lights on and the others followed suit.

"Where are we going to stop?" Michelle asked.

"I can think of no better place than the Schnurberg parking lot. It should certainly shut down business for the night. Might as well stick it to them any chance we get."
"Sounds good to me!"

26

As expected, Schnurberg's management called the police within five minutes of the group's arrival. The three security officers for the store stayed inside the glass entryway and stared out at the crowd, which was growing again. Bonnie lost all track of how many there were, but the parking lot was full. She, Michelle, and Amber took up a spot near the corner of Gravois and Hampton. When the first officer came to talk to them, Bonnie stepped onto the property occupied by the Metro Bus station.

"Are you Bonnie Rose?" the officer asked.

"I am."

"I'm Lieutenant Ray. We have a complaint from Schnurberg's that your group is trespassing."

"Maybe we are waiting for the bus?" Michelle said and smiled. The lieutenant was not amused.

"We won't be here too long," Bonnie said. "I recognize that we are an inconvenience for Schnurberg's. I feel bad about that."

"There is a park just across the road if you need somewhere to rest, although your group cannot spend the night there without the proper permits. Those usually take a couple days to process."

"What do you recommend?"

"I think dispersing the group would be the safest. Rush hour is coming up pretty quick and you simply can't stay here until it's over. People are going to need to get in this lot."

"Again, an inconvenience to an organization that danced around the union to throw out an entire warehouse full of employees. I'm sure you like your union," Amber said.

"Look," Ray said and glanced back at the crowd, "I get what you all are doing. Officially, I have a job to do, and the people at the top of our pay system are the ones that you are marching against. Can you see where this causes a problem for us?"

"Sure do," Bonnie said. "Those are the same people who packed the homeless out into a quarry in the middle of nowhere. They also refuse to fully fund any social program, including the police department. Meanwhile, they want to drop forty million on making the city look prettier in hopes of drawing in developers."

Lieutenant Ray sighed and looked at his partner.

"Bonnie!" Giant said, emerging from the crowd. Tiny was right behind him, and both officers took a defensive stance with such a big guy running their way. "One of Esther's friends just called me. She said they reserved all the pavilions at Tower Grove Park for us. Apparently, they know the right people, because they secured an overnight permit for tonight, too."

Michelle was tapping on her phone and said, "It's a little over four miles from here if we go Gravois to Kingshighway."

"Officer!" yelled a man in a tan outfit with a blue badge stitched on it. "I'm head of security for this Schnurberg's location. I demand to know when you are going to start arresting these people for trespassing."

"I'm giving them… two hours to vacate the premises."

"Two hours?! They need to be gone right now. They are breaking the law."

"Technically," Giant said, "three people went in to buy a pack of gum. They have the receipt."

"Ah, so they are customers," Michelle said. "Is there a limit to how many people a customer can have with them on a visit?"

"I don't believe our policy directly addresses that," the guard said, "but I'm positive that this would exceed a reasonable interpretation of any such policy."

"I'll be back in two hours, Ms. Rose," Ray said. "Please be gone."

"Understood," Bonnie said and smiled.

"All units return to the precinct," Ray said into the radio strapped to his shoulder. He nodded to Bonnie and got back in his car.

"I'm allowed to detain anyone breaking the law until a police officer arrives," the security guard said and pulled a pair of handcuffs from his belt. "I can't get all of you, but I can hold four or five. I'll make examples of you!"

"I don't think I'll let you arrest us today," Bonnie said, but the man stepped forward and slapped a cuff on her right wrist.

"Words won't get you anywhere other than my holding cell," he said. "Now give me your other hand."

"Fine," Bonnie said and put out her left wrist. "I'll do what you want, but you aren't going to like what comes next."

"Strike the shepherd, and the sheep will scatter," he said and snapped the cuffs shut. "You are smart not to resist."

"You done?" she asked.

"*You* are the one who is done!"

"I'll take that bet," she said and pulled her wrists apart. The chain went taught. She stretched her hands further apart, causing the chains to shutter and then some links began to separate at the welded seams. Marchers that were near Bonnie stared. They began elbowing their neighbors and the people at the edge of the crowd in the Schnurberg's parking lot tried to get a better look.

The chain gave in an instant, and the weakest link shot away to Bonnie's right. Alicia happened to be walking toward the street, but looked up just as the link reached her. No one could tell how she did it. Her hand was a blur, and she caught the misshapen metal with a backhand swipe.

At that moment, the guard pulled a small club from his belt and reached back to swing at Bonnie. Instead, Michelle grabbed it and yanked him backward by the wrist. Erv was close by, took hold of the man's belt and lifted him in the air like a pro wrestler about to body slam someone.

"No!" Bonnie yelled and Erv glanced at her. Instead, he tossed the man into the crowd. The people were packed tight, and the guard began floating across their outstretched hands. "Legion! Don't do it!"

"We are not doing anything," Legion said in a soft, even voice.

Three young men at the edge of the crowd were watching the guard float away, but they heard Bonnie yell out about Legion. They looked at each other with a puzzled look.

"Did she call us Legion?" one of them asked.

"I think so. That's a cool name."

"We are Legion," a deep, firm voice said, and their eyes widened, thinking their friend had said it.

"Yeah," the second one said, "We are Legion!"

"We are Legion!" they both shouted. "We are Legion! We are Legion!"

The crowd around them picked up the chant and soon it spread across the parking lot. Everyone from the old to the young adopted the phrase, and Erv smiled. Michelle started laughing. The rest of Bonnie's team looked pleased as they gathered around her.

"Fine," Bonnie said with confident resignation. She pinched the handcuff on her right wrist between her left forefinger and thumb. The metal broke as if she were snapping her fingers through air. She repeated the motion on the other wrist and rubbed them while she thought. "Let's go."

Bonnie did not look for feedback from her friends, instead walking to the center of Gravois Road. She ignored the honks from oncoming cars. The rest of the marchers were close behind her and traffic on Gravois Road came to a complete stop for the next forty-five minutes.

An hour after that, they made it to Tower Grove Park. The chant of 'We are Legion' continued for the entirety of that leg of the march. As they turned into the driveway for the park, the blast of alternative rock filled the air. Bonnie could see a stage ahead to her left and a row of food trucks directly ahead of her. It looked like a concert was going on, but the music's volume fell, and the people in the park began cheering when they saw the marchers.

"Here they come!" shouted the man behind the podium. The other five people on the podium were wearing tank tops and they came down to greet the walkers. "We did an Eagle Call at the end of our show this morning, and this is the result! We have a great group of Weirdos out here today. Everyone grab some food and take a load off."

"Glad you got that podium just in time, Rizz," said the tank top guy with the beard. He motioned for Bonnie to come up on the stage. "Hey everyone, Jeff Burton here. I'm talking to Bonnie Rose, the organizer of this march. What made you want to do this?"

"Well, it was the right thing to do," Bonnie said. "I was lucky enough to get a chance at life, when I could have ended up in a much worse situation. When I found out about the homeless people being forced into a camp in an old quarry, well, I had to do something."

"That's awesome," Jeff said.

"But I certainly couldn't have done it without help from my friends. This is one outstanding crew!"

Rafe took the air next and spoke with Giant and Tiny, although the big man didn't say anything. Moon talked to Michelle, Amber, and Ryan. Lern talked to Erv, Esther, and Alicia. Then, Bonnie and her friends spread out to talk to walkers and volunteers with an alternative rock soundtrack in the background.

27

"Ah, Lieutenant Ray," Bonnie said as she walked across the crisp grass of Tower Grove Park. She felt rested and ready for the final leg of the march. She didn't know what waited at the end of that day, but she was confident they could handle it. "Good to see you again. I think we have all the permits to be here."

"Yes," Ray said with a smile. "Your group is good to go until dusk tonight. I'm guessing you won't be staying here another night though."

"You'd be right about that."

"Just a heads up though, the mayor has instructed the chief to have anyone caught in the park after dark arrested."

"Don't you all have anything better to do than arrest homeless people?" a woman yelled from a small gathering to Bonnie's right. Bonnie recognized her as one of the women from the quarry.

"We have a lot of better things to do, actually," Ray said. "However, the people on high have to play politics and that, as they say, runs downhill. Fact is that we are fully expecting things to escalate before the day ends and we are hoping that your group plans to stay peaceful."

"We do. Although it will be hard to say what will happen if the group is attacked."

"Let's hope that doesn't happen then," Ray said.

"Hey! Lieutenant!" a man called out from a food truck parked along the driveway. "Are your guys hungry? I've got plenty of breakfast burritos."

"I'm sure there will be some takers," Ray said. "Hey, Blankenship, let the other guys know that breakfast is available if they want it."

"I'm on it," Blankenship said.

"I knew you would be," Ray said before turning back to Bonnie. "Just do me a favor and keep everyone safe."

"I'll do my best," Bonnie said and shook the lieutenant's hand. Ray took a cup of coffee from the food truck, but that was all. It didn't take long for him to be back in his car and pulling away from the park.

Several news trucks were set up along Magnolia Street between Tower Grove Park and the Missouri Botanical Gardens. The local outlets were accounted for, and a few major networks were now on the scene. CNN, MSNBC, and BBC were up and interviewing marchers. Esther and Erv had volunteered to speak with reporters. Bonnie was grateful for that offer.

"So," Giant said to Bonnie, "apparently not everyone in the mayor's office is a big fan of her. Word has just come in that she is ordering the streets blocked off around city hall. She is going to issue a statement saying that the marchers are likely to damage and loot downtown. She is also going to call on the Metropolitan Police to do their job and break up this dangerous demonstration."

"That's rich," Ryan said. "She thinks we are dangerous?"

"Dangerous to her career, maybe," Amber said. "I just hope she doesn't put enough pressure on the chief of police to make him do something to us."

"I think he'll do the right thing," Bonnie said. "We need to get moving, though. Come with me."

Bonnie jogged toward the news trucks and the reporters saw her coming. They broke away from Esther and went to meet Bonnie.

"Bonnie!" called out the reporter from CNN, but Bonnie put up her hands and came to a stop.

"I'm not going to answer questions right now. Turn on the cameras," she said and waited for the cameraman to point to her. "I want everyone to know that we are going to go up Grand to Park. Then, we'll go from Park to 14th. If anyone wants to join us, they are welcome. The mayor is apparently in the process of blockading city hall off from us as if this is some sort of street war. Also, business owners and residents in the area should know that we have not done any damage so far and we will not be doing any when we get downtown. Do not fear us. Join us!"

"We are Legion!" a group of people yelled from behind Bonnie. She turned to look at them, but she knew they were speaking on their own, and they didn't mean the real Legion.

"We are Legion, they say," the reporter said. "I can't think of a better chant for your group."

"Sounds like the masses have spoken," Bonnie said and smiled. She did not give them a chance to ask her anything, instead starting to walk along Magnolia toward Grand.

"She is walking," Legion said in a voice that all the walkers could hear, though they did not know who said it. They all thought it was just someone nearby, and they started after her.

Bonnie's call for more support on TV worked. Morning radio shows picked up the request, and soon people were hopping out of their cars along the route and joining the group. They were now blocking the entire width of the road and stretching out over a couple blocks.

"It's going to be a flood at city hall," Michelle said.

"When we get to 14th and Clark," Bonnie said, "I want you, Amber, and Ryan to split off to the right. I'll stop at the intersection and try to divide people up. Erv, Esther, Giant, Tiny, and Alicia can go left."

"Sounds like a good plan to me," Michelle said. "You want me to go back and let the team know?"

"Nah," Bonnie said. "Legion can handle that, I think."

About an hour later, they reached the southwest corner of the city hall block. Enterprise Center and Stiefel Theater stood to the west. Bonnie turned and smiled back at the group who slowed for a moment, but quickly understood what she wanted when she began gently waving her arms and pointing both ways. The rest of her friends were right there and took the lead of their assigned flank.

The scene looked similar to what Bonnie had expected. The city workers had been busy, setting up concrete barriers like the ones used to divide highways around the entire block. Chain link fencing had been installed on top of those. It looked like a fortress. Only the entrance to the parking lot along 14th street had been left open, but it had a gate plus two dump trucks parked sideways across it. Legion had become more of a threat to the mayor than Bonnie had imagined.

Two box trucks pulled up and parked in front of Enterprise Center. Several workers came out of the trucks, opened the roll up doors, and revealed hundreds of cases of water. Bonnie nodded, knowing that support was only going to grow for this movement.

"Now what?" Amber asked, having walked back around to Bonnie's position once her flank was in place.

"We wait," Bonnie said. "The mayor has to address us at some point. I'm glad I wore sensible shoes."

"You're hilarious," Amber said, shaking her head before walking away.

The group milled around along the barrier for the next hour, when the mayor made her first response. A dozen black SUVs pulled up and began driving through the group. They were going slow, but people moved. Some beat on the hood and sides of the vehicles. Bonnie knew those vehicles were meant to incite a negative reaction.

"I'm not moving," Giant said with Tiny at his side. "I don't think they'll run me down, and I can probably just flip them over with the help of Legion."

Bonnie heard him, even though she was half a block away. "None of that, Giant! We cannot be the first to react."

"Fine, but that's no fun," he said.

"I have a suggestion," a man in a worn-out jean jacket said as he approached Bonnie. "I'm one of the homeless who slipped through the mayor's net back when she rounded us up for the quarry. I served in Vietnam, and I think these trucks are going to make something bad happen. I've seen riots erupt from less."

"Go on."

"Can I borrow your phone?"

"Sure," Bonnie said, handing over her phone. His blue eyes sparkled despite the rest of him looking totally fatigued. He dialed a number and spoke in a voice just above a whisper. When he was done, he handed it back.

"You won't have to worry about the trucks for much longer," he said.

"Nothing violent I hope," she said.

"Never."

"What's your name?"

"My name is Brad," he said with a smile and extended his hand. "I appreciate what you are doing here, and I look forward to having my friends back."

With that, he melted back into the crowd, and she didn't see him again. The trucks kept circling the block, and she noticed marchers drifting away after the trucks went by. The mayor was probably watching this from her office window, hoping people would disperse if they felt threatened.

More than fifty people moved away from the barriers and out of the way of the trucks over the next thirty minutes, but then Brad's idea came to fruition. The rumble of motors could be heard from blocks away and a wave of energy ran through the crowd. When the first ten motorcycles came around the corner, people cheered. The Freedom Riders had arrived.

The riders drove into the crowd, which parted easily. The SUVs had been making a counter-clockwise circle, so the bikers went the opposite way. They pulled into a crosswalk and waited for the next truck. It pulled up to them and the riders stared at the driver with a blank expression.

Other riders started blocking off the intersections, essentially creating a safe loop around city hall for the marchers. Six more riders came in behind the last black SUV and urged it forward. One by one, the SUVs were funneled out. The crowd began chanting, "We are Legion!"

The chanting grew louder, and some of the marchers started rattling the chain link fence. Bonnie was sure the noise could be heard all the way to the river. Then, she saw Lieutenant Ray again. He was running across the parking lot inside the barrier, headed directly for her. Bonnie stepped up to meet him.

"The mayor has issued an order to, as she said, 'neutralize' any marcher that crosses the barrier. Most of us will not enforce that, but I'm afraid it will only take one to set off a full blown fight."

"We are going to remain peaceful," Bonnie said.

"You've got a lot more people now than when you started. Just like one officer who does something dumb can start a big problem, a marcher who does something stupid can do the same. The chief has said we are here to protect city property and employees, not attack a crowd. Like I said, though, not everyone agrees with him."

"So, is she going to address us?"

"I don't think so. She's hoping that this thing will turn into a powder keg that she can ignite. I wouldn't be surprised if she sent people into your crowd to rile people up."

"Sounds about right," Bonnie said, looking at the marchers and thinking that she only knew a handful of the thousands that were there. "Are the other city officials in the building on board with the mayor?"

"I don't think so, but no one is talking to her."

"Thanks, Lieutenant," she said. "I will come up with a plan on our side."

"Good luck," he said and ran back across the lot.

"We are *Legion!*" echoed through the downtown streets as she tried to think of a plan. Feeding the crowd would become an issue soon, and she knew this couldn't go on beyond the day.

"We can handle this," she heard Legion say. Before she could respond, the crowd began to press in on the blockade. The concrete barriers started to tip and slide, the chain link bending a little more with each forward push.

"This is *our* city hall, not yours!" yelled a man with a bullhorn near the front steps of the grand old building. "We are Legion!"

The mayor rushed out the front door of city hall. She pulled open the door to a police car parked nearby and grabbed the microphone.

"Turn it on," she instructed the officer inside the car. "You are all hereby ordered to disperse by my instruction. I will tell the chief of police to begin arresting any and all protestors blocking any street in ten minutes. I am the duly elected leader of this city, and you will respect that! This hall will be protected by my police force by whatever means are necessary."

The chief looked at her after this last line. The total disbelief on his face was hard to miss. Somehow, the mayor believed the police would act as her personal army, but the chief would not stand by for that.

"Now, you have nine more minutes to clear the area, or you will be removed!"

The chief took the radio from his shoulder and drew in a deep breath.

"Attention all officers, this is Colonel Hampton. You will stand down. I repeat, stand down."

"What?!" the mayor yelled. "You serve at my leisure, Colonel Hampton. You will do as I say."

Hampton looked at her for a moment longer and then walked toward the parking lot to the south of city hall. The chanting escalated and the barrier began to shake again. The mayor covered her ears, but the look of fury on her face was plenty to let everyone know she wasn't scared.

A man in a gray suit got out of a sedan near the front entrance of Enterprise Center and walked toward the gate with the dump trucks. He was carrying a leather folder and had three other men with him, but they easily maneuvered through the crowd. When they reached the gate, the officer responsible for the gate slid it open without a word and closed it again behind them. The marchers did not try to push through.

As the mayor fumed, the four men walked across the parking lot. She saw them come around the corner of city hall and smiled. Her reinforcements had arrived in the form of the president of the board of aldermen.

"President Bonner," she said. "It is good to see you. The chief is refusing to follow my instructions, and I am about to relieve him of his duties."

"A relief of duty is exactly why I am here," Bonner said.

"Good!" she said and looked at Colonel Hampton, who stood with his arms crossed.

"This action is long overdue," Bonner said and pulled a document from his folder. "Mayor, the board of aldermen for the city of St. Louis met an hour ago. We have reviewed your actions in the recent days along with some recently acquired documents pertaining to the quarry camp for the homeless. Needless to say, that project has turned into a funnel of money for some of your top supporters. We believe you are no longer acting in the interest of the citizens of St. Louis. The board has completed a unanimous vote of no confidence in your abilities. You are hereby removed from authority."

"You can't do that!"

"We can, and we did," Bonner said. "Colonel Hampton, please come over here."

The chief had been watching from his spot twenty feet away, smiling at the development.

"What can I do for you, President Bonner?"

"I need two of your officers to escort our former mayor safely to her home. I want two officers left to guard her home for the next seventy-two hours."

"I have the right to go back to my office," she said. "I have personal belongings in there."

"Your office will be cleaned out by city personnel and your items delivered to your home."

The rattling of the chain link fences came to an abrupt stop, and a stiff breeze blew through downtown. The sudden silence caused the group of politicians to look around. Hampton was pleased.

Two officers in a marked police car pulled up alongside the ousted mayor. Bonner opened the back door and gestured for her to get in.

"You want me to leave in the backseat of a police car?" she said, glaring at him.

"It's what you are going to do, yes."

She huffed and slid into the back seat. The car pulled away, and the dump trucks moved when the car approached. The crowd parted, and motorcycles left their spot blocking the intersection when the squad car came through. People began chanting 'We are Legion' again and the mayor frowned at them with her arms crossed. Bonnie watched from her corner of the block, but somehow felt different.

"How do you feel, Michelle?" Bonnie said, but there was no response. That was when she realized that the difference she was feeling was the silence in her own mind. She couldn't hear what anyone else was thinking and her body felt strangely relaxed.

The crowd chanted louder and louder, but something drew Bonnie's attention to her left. She wound through the crowd and emerged near the Enterprise Center. A woman of about sixty was standing at one of the service doors to the stadium in a pair of worn out overalls. She smiled at Bonnie.

"Our work is done here," she said, but Bonnie could hear her perfectly over the crowd.

"You're leaving, then?"

"This group is your new Legion. Use that power wisely. When people work together for the greater good, nothing is impossible."

"I thought you only left when we decided that we didn't want your help anymore."

"It is a mutual thing, remember. Both sides must be interested for the work to continue. We are no longer needed here. Stay strong. You have great things ahead of you, Bonnie Rose."

Bonnie accepted Legion's decision and watched the woman go through the door. She was sure she would never hear that voice again, but she hoped she would see the results of Legion's work elsewhere. Watching the news would never be the same.

The crowd started chanting, "*We are Legion! We are Legion! We are Legion!*"

The End